I0547715

Leather Home

I.G. Frederick

"Theresa" — Richard admits to boorish behavior, but Theresa has no use for his apology. Then, he persuades her to accept a ride home from him and proves his integrity.

"Richard" — Theresa fascinated Richard from the first time he saw her. But how does he convince her to consider more than a casual relationship with another dominant?

"Searching" — Two dominants love each other, but need someone who submits to them both. Just how far will young Jesse go to serve the lovely Lady Theresa?

"Jesse" — Jesse finds the perfect Mistress, the woman he trained all his life to serve. Unfortunately, her husband also finds Jesse attractive.

I.G. Frederick trades words for cash, specializing in erotic fiction and poetry since 2001. Her erotic short stories appear in Hustler Fantasies, Forum, Foreplay, and Desire Presents, as well as electronic, audio, and print anthologies. Her novels receive high praise from readers, critics, and other authors.

A FemDom, Ms. Frederick, owns the man she adores. Although dominant in the rest of his life, he demonstrates his love by serving as her submissive. Ms. Frederick often writes about finding love in BDSM relationships from the authority of one enjoying that for almost a decade.

http://eroticawriter.net/

Sometimes love takes us strange places before it brings us home

Leather Home

I.G. Frederick

Author of Switch & Family Dynamics

Leather Home

ISBN: 9781937471378

Pussy Cat Press
http://pussycatpress.com/publisher.html/
P.O. Box 19764
Portland OR 97280

Table of Contents

Theresa

By I.G. Frederick

One pair of eyes caressed Theresa's skin, but she couldn't sort through the crowd to figure out who they belonged to. She concentrated on the whip in her hand and the naked boy bound in front of her on the cross, staying alert for those who strayed close enough to her scene that they risked a painful leather kiss.

She hated playing in public – too many lookie lous; too many asshole Doms hitting on her, thinking because she was tiny they could make her kneel; and too many newbie idiots who didn't know enough to stay out of range of a six-foot signal whip.

Raising her whip above her head to avoid yet another careless voyeur, she added one more stripe to the dozens of welts across Jon's back and stepped closer, looping her whip across her palm. She released the winch to lower the cuffs holding his hands above his head and pressed against him, using her body weight to keep him from falling backwards. Removing the cuffs, she dropped them into the small duffle by his feet. He could clean them, and the whip, tomorrow.

"Can you walk?"

He pressed his lips together, then nodded.

Theresa slipped the whip into the bag, zipped it, and pulled the strap up over her shoulder. She put her right arm around Jon's waist and held his left hand in hers, guiding him to the chairs surrounding the snack table. When she had him settled onto a towel-covered seat, she retrieved a bottle of water and a paper cup full of trail mix and sat down next to him. While Jon munched and sipped, Theresa stroked his soft, greying hair.

A tall, muscular man with dark brown, almost black hair and a diamond in his left earlobe, plopped into the chair beside her and stretched out his long, leather clad legs. "I take it you're a service top?"

Theresa stared at him.

"It's obvious, you gave that boy everything he wanted."

She grimaced. "It's his birthday and he begged for the privilege of buying me a new dress and taking me to this party."

The man stared down the low-cut neckline of the figure-hugging red dress Jon had purchased. "And, what did he do to deserve such a delectable present?"

"Not that it's any of your business, but he cleans my house every week, does my nails, washes my hair." Theresa glared at him.

"Oh, you're a pro?"

"I take it you've never met a FemDom before." She spat out. "Let me guess, you're an online bottom and this party is your first real life experience." She turned in her seat so her back was to the interloper.

"My apologies." The deep voice penetrated the techno music that set the beat for the players in the dungeon.

She ignored him.

"I know, and am friends with, many FemDoms. I was just hoping, despite the evidence, that you weren't one."

He rose and stepped in front of her, squatting down between her and Jon. "I also do not wish to interfere with this man's aftercare. But perhaps you would consider allowing me to buy you dinner some night this coming week to make up for my boorish behavior."

She leaned away from him, as far back as the chair would allow, and stared, taken aback by his audacity and, she had to admit to herself, his rugged good looks. "If you do not leave me alone, I will ask the Dungeon Monitor to eject you from this event."

Every muscle in his face turned down and the sadness in his rich brown eyes almost made her reconsider. "My apologies." He stood and walked away.

Theresa expelled the breath in her lungs that she hadn't realized she was holding.

"I'm sorry, Mistress," Jon whispered.

She pulled him into her arms. "It's not your fault."

Theresa stepped into the back room and scanned the crowd of men and women, most wearing street clothes, a few in fetish garb. Seeing no sign of the boy who had courted her online and promised to meet her at the munch, she slipped into a corner booth, hoping to remain unnoticed. She saw none of her friends and no one she cared to get acquainted with. In the past few years, she'd become a recluse, avoiding community events, only playing with a few close friends at their homes or hers, accepting service from a married man whose wife couldn't understand his needs.

Numerous online conversations ended when she suggested a real life meeting, or worse they made a date and stood her up. She expected that outcome tonight and positioned herself where she could watch the door in hopes of seeing someone she knew who would enjoy sharing a drink with her.

But the only familiar face that entered the dimly lit, wood-panelled room was the prick from the party she took Jon to for his birthday. Theresa snatched up the menu and held it in front of her face, pretending to read the wine list.

"Mind if I join you?" He stood, blocking her ability to exit the booth.

"Yes, I do. Very much." She set the menu down on the table and tried to signal the harried waiter entering from the bar with a tray full of drinks. "I'm waiting to meet someone."

"Birthday boy?"

"It really is none of your business."

He bowed his head. "I know. And, I know you don't owe me the time of day. But I would really like an opportunity to make amends for the other night and let you see that I'm really not an asshole."

"I don't care one way or the other. I would just like you to stop bothering me."

"Look. I'll make a deal with you. Let me buy you a drink, right here at the munch where everyone can see us. If I can't convince you by the time you finish it that I'm not a jerk, I promise to never approach you again without specific invitation."

The waiter chose that moment to appear at the table. Before she could say anything, the man ordered a whiskey sour.

"Rum. Neat." She could down that quickly and be rid of the schmuck.

The waiter disappeared before she could specify label. She sighed, knowing she would get a cheap, well brand.

Unfortunately, she hadn't taken into account the time it would take the single waiter, trying to serve a few dozen kinksters, to return with the drink. The son of a bitch sat down opposite her and leaned across the varnished, faux petrified wood table.

"I will apologize one more time for my inexcusable behavior the other night. I was so mesmerized by your beauty that I wanted desperately for you to be a submissive, or at least a switch, so I could court you. I was incredibly obnoxious. I made some insulting assumptions based on witnessing a scene between two people I knew nothing about." He hung his head. "And, here I am adding insult to injury by insisting you hear me out." He took a deep breath and slid out of the booth.

"Thank you for accepting my drink." He put a ten and a five on the table. "Please tell the waiter to keep the change and I hope your date will enjoy the whiskey sour. Since I can't convince myself I haven't been a dickhead toward you, I know there's no hope of convincing you. I will keep my promise." He turned on his heel and trudged toward the exit.

Theresa stared after him eyes wide, mouth open. When the waiter set the drinks on the table, she handed him the money, put the shot glass to her lips, tilted her head back, and swallowed, letting the amber liquid burn its way down her throat. She shook her head. Well, at least she could hope the bastard learned his lesson and wouldn't afflict himself on any other unwilling women at future events.

After half an hour, she downed the whiskey sour as well and strode out of the restaurant into the cold rain. Alone as usual.

T

A week later, Theresa couldn't believe she had agreed to come to the munch again in hopes of meeting yet another boy who sounded promising online. She swore to herself if this one didn't show up, she would close her account and just stop trying.

As she reached for the door to the back room, a long, muscular arm snaked in front of her hand and pulled it open. She looked up to see the handsome asshole holding the door ajar, standing as far away from her as it would allow. He nodded, but didn't speak. She shuddered and turned away from him, venturing into the room looking in vain for the man who had only sent her a photo the night before.

When she slid into the same booth, the waiter, balancing a loaded tray, dropped off a shot of amber liquid. "Rum, neat. From the gentleman."

Theresa sighed and took a sip, enjoying the rich smooth taste. At least he ordered the good stuff. Out of the corner of her eye, she saw the man talking to Angelo and almost dropped the glass. She hadn't seen Angelo in years, but had no desire to approach him while the degenerate was in the same proximity.

Fortunately, Angelo spotted her and, after exchanging a few words with the pilgarlic, approached her booth. "Theresa, darling. It's so good to see you out in the community again." Angelo kissed her fingers when she proffered her hand. "You look lovely as ever. How have you been?"

Theresa smiled."Not really participating in the community. Just here for a safe place to meet someone I corresponded with online and who's apparently stood me up."

Angelo slid into the booth across from her. "Still haven't found your pet?"

She shook her head. Angelo had been her mentor when she first entered the scene. "You set high standards. Haven't found anyone who lives up to them."

He laughed. "You actually met someone who lives up to them the other night. Just the wrong orientation. And, so smitten with your gorgeous self, he apparently made a complete jackass of himself. I offered to introduce Richard to you, who by the way I also mentored, but he believes he has eradicated any possibility of even becoming friends."

She nodded, but before she could speak, Angelo continued. "However, as a favor to me, I would appreciate you giving him a second chance, at least for a few hours. I'm only in town for the evening and I haven't seen either of you in a very long while."

Theresa looked around the room once more to prove that her date was a no show.

"He promises to be on his very best behavior."

She sighed and shrugged her shoulders.

Angelo turned to the dolt who leaned against the wall by the exit and nodded. The man strode over to the table as if he owned the joint. Theresa wished she could change her mind.

When he reached the table, he bowed from the waist. "Pleased to make your acquaintance, Lady Theresa. Thanks for allowing me to join you and our mutual mentor."

Angelo shifted further into the booth making room for Richard to sit on his side of the table. Theresa downed her drink and waved her empty glass at the waiter who brought her another and took orders from the two Doms sitting across from her. Even seated, they towered over her and she hated feeling vulnerable. She ignored Richard as much as possible, grateful that Angelo steered the conversation in neutral directions.

The room emptied over the hours and finally the waiter informed them that he needed to close up. Theresa pushed herself out of the booth and almost fell over. *Should NOT have ordered that fourth drink.* She looked up at the two men's concerned faces. "I'll be fine. Just stood up too quickly."

Angelo gave her what she always called his *No Way* look – one eyebrow raised above the other, one fist on his hip. "You're drunk. How did you get here?"

"Walked over from the office. I can take a cab home."

Richard offered her his hand. "Please, Theresa. Let me drive you home. Least I can do."

Only the thought of trying to find a taxi in the rain when she could barely stand, made that thought appealing. She looked to Angelo who nodded. With a sigh, she took Richard's hand and had to force herself not to jerk it back. She stared up into his dark eyes and stifled a gasp. He just grinned.

Theresa let him steady her as they walked out of the restaurant. His touch made her melt. In the parking lot, she hugged Angelo goodbye and Richard handed her into his Acura. Except for giving him her address, Theresa didn't speak until Richard pulled up in front of her condo building. "I can manage from here."

He maneuvered into a parking space. "I'm not so sure about that. Please let me help you."

She took a deep breath. She had to admit, he was hot. And if they had sex, she could just chalk it up to being drunk. "I guess."

Richard helped her out of the car and kept his arm around her as they approached the building. He caught her keys when she dropped them trying to find the lock and helped her into the vestibule. He didn't try to kiss her on the elevator, probably because of the security cameras. When they reached her unit, he unlocked the door and guided her to the leather sofa in her living room. She was grateful to sit down so the room would stop spinning.

"Theresa, you are without a doubt the most beautiful woman I have ever met. I would very much like to have sex with you, but you're obviously intoxicated so all I can do is give you my number and beg you to call me when you're sober." He handed her a business card. The numbers were too blurry to read. He kissed the back of her hand, dropped her keys on the coffee table, and let himself out of the condo.

Theresa stared at the door, her mouth half open. She should have known. Anyone Angelo mentored would never take advantage of someone incapable of giving consent. She tilted sideways, brought her feet up onto the cushions and fell asleep, still clothed and wearing her boots.

𝒯

In the morning, it took a shower and three cups of coffee before Theresa felt normal. She knew better than to have more than two drinks. Standing in front of the picture window that looked out over the river, trying to comb the tangles out of her waist-length hair, Theresa spotted the small white square sticking out from under the couch. She picked it up and turned it over. Obviously his scene card, it only had "Sir

Richard," an email address, and a cell number. She dropped it on the coffee table.

The card sat there for a week before Theresa decided to call. Of course, she got voice mail. "Hi. It's Theresa. Just wanted to thank you for the ride home the other night. And for being a gentleman." She hung up, feeling stupid, and tossed the card in the recycle bin.

Two days later, an unfamiliar number appeared on her cell while she let Jon worship her feet as a reward for cleaning her condo. "Hello?"

"Hi, Theresa, it's Richard. Sorry I didn't get back to you sooner, but I was down in the Bay Area this week. Would you consider going out to dinner with me?"

"Why?"

He chuckled. "Because I'm hoping you find me a little attractive and a bit intriguing and that you might consider having sex with me."

Well at least he was honest. "But, I'm a sadist."

"So am I."

"I've never submitted to anyone."

"Neither have I. But, we could have vanilla sex, no bondage, no pain, no power exchange."

She tilted her head. "Vanilla sex?" She watched the tips of Jon's ears redden. "I've never had vanilla sex."

"You're kidding?"

Theresa shook her head, even though Richard couldn't see her. "No. My first lover was kinky and he gave me a paddle as a present on our second date. In fact, he's the one who introduced me to Angelo."

Silence.

Jon looked up, his face red. "I should get home, Mistress. May I get dressed to leave?"

She nodded.

"Wow," Richard said. "I've never met anyone ... I mean, most people ... what ..." The phone went silent again. "I don't suppose you'd like to try it once?"

She shrugged. *I guess vanilla sex is better than none.* Aloud, she said, "I don't know. Maybe." He would call when she was all hot and bothered by foot worship from a man who could go home and fuck his vanilla wife.

"So, how about dinner?"

C

Dinner was expensive and delicious and it could have been fish and chips at Burgerville. The only thing she saw was Richard's muscular chest under his black silk shirt. The only thing she smelled was the leather of his pants and the testosterone that rolled off him. The only thing she wanted to taste was his tongue in her mouth, even if she couldn't bite it.

He kissed her fingers during the appetizers, licked her neck during dinner, and nibbled on her ear through dessert. By the time the bill arrived, she was panting.

"Your place or mine?" He handed her into his Acura.

For some reason, the idea of sex without power exchange in her own bed was a real turn off. "Yours."

Richard owned a house in the west hills. After hanging their coats on a rack by the front door, he led Theresa up a carpeted staircase to a bedroom furnished in dark wood and leather. The covers pulled back on the king-sized bed revealed silky black sheets. Stepping up behind her, he wrapped his arms around her waist and dragged his tongue from the base of her neck to below her ear. "Should we get naked?"

She turned in his arms and looked up into his dark eyes. "No bondage? No pain? No power exchange? What exactly are we going to do?"

He laughed. "Well, see, I have this thing called a penis and you have this thing called a vagina and I would like to stick my penis in your vagina."

She gave him an exasperated *sheesh*. "I know that much."

"Wasn't sure. Don't know much about FemDom sex. Just don't expect me to ask for permission to come."

"At least warn me?"

"Sure." He tangled his fingers into her hair. She tilted her head back and he pressed his lips against hers. Her breathing, which had calmed to normal during the ride home, picked up its pace again. She parted her lips and his tongue explored the inside of her mouth. Her hands roamed across his broad chest and she found herself undoing the buttons of his shirt, eager to eliminate any barrier between her fingers and his skin.

His nipples were hard and she longed to bite them. She restrained herself and tweaked them with her thumbs instead. He inhaled sharply. She grinned. Causing a reaction was half the fun of hurting someone.

Richard's mouth moved from hers and his lips burned her neck. He reached back and slowly pulled down the zipper of her black sheath, revealing her naked torso, and gasped again. Pulling back far enough that he could slip her dress off her shoulders, he stared at her small firm breasts and the silky, dark curls between her legs. He ran one finger along the top of her thigh-highs. "Mind leaving those on for me?"

She shrugged and stepped out of the dress pooled at her feet. "As long as you're naked."

He chuckled and kicked off his shoes and pulled off his shirt, tossing it at the leather easy chair in the corner, then unbuckled his belt and unbuttoned his slacks. Slowly, he lowered the zipper. She stared, waiting. He let the pants drop to the floor with a clunk of wallet and keys. The tip of his hard cock peered out above the tops of his black bikini underpants and she sighed.

"What's wrong?"

"Just thinking how much I would enjoy torturing that."

"Sorry. Could say the same thing about your pretty, pert tits." He reached out and ran one finger from her chest to her nipple. She gasped.

He slipped off the briefs, grabbed a condom out of a nightstand drawer, and flopped on his back on the bed. "But, I'm sure you can think of other things to do with this." He rolled a red rubber over his prick. "Ones that don't hurt."

She grinned and planted her palms on either side of his legs, crawling up him until her pussy was just above his cock. "Torture doesn't have to involve pain."

"There's a difference between torment and teasing." He raised his hips so his glans nudged her lips, then dropped back. "And, two can play the latter game."

Theresa sank down on his dick and her eyes rolled back in her head. He fit perfectly, just thick enough to massage her g-spot. She rose up on her knees and slid down again. Richard reached up with one hand to tickle her nipple with his fingers. With his other thumb he massaged her clit. She clenched her cunt muscles. He moaned and pushed his hips up, plunging deeper into her. Bracing herself against his chest, her thumbs on his nipples, she pushed herself up and down. Richard increased pressure on her clit until the building tension shattered, her entire body shaking, her pussy clamping down on his dick.

"Consider this your warning," he growled. He grabbed her hips and furiously pumped up and down until he groaned and she could feel him pulsing inside her.

She collapsed onto his chest and he embraced her. When he slipped out, he rolled them both over so they lay on their sides, facing each other, chests pressed together, arms wrapped around each other.

When she finally caught her breath, she said: "Wow. I didn't know 'nilla sex could be that good."

"Chemistry, my dear. If you have it, any sex is fabulous. If you don't ..."

She had to agree with him. Despite Jon's devotion to serving her and his masochism, she had never wanted sex with him, even if he had been single. She limited him to foot worship as much because she could close her eyes and pretend someone else licked her toes as because that's where Jon's wife had drawn the line.

He put one hand on her cheek. "But, sex that good deserves more than a one-night stand, doncha you think?"

She wrinkled her nose. "Friends with benefits, maybe. But, I need someone in service to me, someone I *can* hurt.

He laughed again. She decided she liked the sound. "So do I. But, I never said anything about monogamy. Who knows, maybe we can find someone who will serve us both."

She shook her head. "Not likely. I'm straight."

He palmed one breast and pushed her on her back so he could lean down and drag his tongue across the other. "Fortunately, I'm not."

Theresa shuddered as much from the thought of Richard ramming into the ass of a boy licking her pussy as the sensation of his wet mouth caressing her nipple. She wrapped her leg around his muscular thigh and rubbed her clit against the hair-covered skin.

Chuckling, he grabbed her ass with his other hand, fondling her cheek. Her breathing, which had never quite slowed to normal, quickened again. "You'd like that, wouldn't you. Me fucking one of your pretty boys in the ass while he licked you? Sucking my jism out of your cunt after you and I fucked?"

He pressed his leg into her, but then pulled away from her. She whimpered, but it was only so he could grab another condom from the drawer. Once sheathed, Richard rolled on top of her and she opened her legs wide. With one hand on either side of her face, he leaned down and kissed her, shoving his tongue into her mouth at the same time he pushed his cock into her cunt.

Wrapping her legs around his waist, she slid her fingers through his long, dark hair, remembering not to stop and grab the strands. Her hands drifted across his powerful shoulders and she slipped under his arms to slide them around his back and pull him closer to her. So, this was the dreaded missionary position. She couldn't understand why folks derided it so. The muscles of his chest massaged her tits, his cock stroked the sensitive walls of her pussy, and his pubic bone rubbed her clit. Awash in sensual waves, her body floated in euphoria even as tension built. Her convulsions, muted by the weight of his body, reverberated through him and she found herself slipping from self identification into a duality she'd never experienced.

They exploded together, the intensity of her cunt's vibrations indistinguishable from the throbbing of his prick. She lost track of when orgasms morphed into aftershocks and her arms slipped from his back unable to maintain enough rigidity to keep them up. Richard kissed her lips, her nose, her forehead, then fell to his side, cradling her head on his shoulder, one arm flung across her chest. They were both panting. She tried to move her mouth, but she couldn't form words.

"Wow is right. I'm guessing you've never tried missionary before."

She managed to nod.

"More where that came from."

"Hmmmmm." She closed her horribly heavy eyes and was vaguely aware of Richard covering her with a sheet and blanket.

ꞆꞆꞆ

Richard

I.G. Frederick

Richard leaned on one elbow, watching the small pert tits of the gorgeous Domme rise and fall as she slept. He'd pulled a blanket over her up to her waist, but couldn't bear to cover those soft mounds of pleasure just yet. Her glorious straight hair, the color of coconut shells, spread across his pillow and surrounded her in a cloud of softness.

Damn. He'd thought if he could just fuck her once, he could get her image out of his head, her soft voice and delicious scent out of his system. But, now he just wanted her more. He couldn't remember the last time he'd had vanilla sex and he'd had to use tremendous control to resist hurting her, but it had still been the most fabulous encounter he'd had with a woman since Ellen left his service three years ago.

When he couldn't keep his eyes open, he settled down next to her, nuzzling her neck and sliding one arm under her beautiful breasts. His last conscious thought was: *Gonna make this work, somehow.*

R

Richard woke to am empty bed. Only a few, stray hairs on his pillow and her tantalizing aroma remained to assure him he hadn't dreamed his blissful encounter with the lovely Lady Theresa. His stomach growled. He couldn't recall a single thing he had eaten for dinner, but he remembered every detail of the hours afterwards – the softness of her skin, the silkiness of her hair, the look of ecstasy on her face when she sat on his cock, the exquisite pleasure of her pussy clamping down on it. The memories made him hard.

He heard the shower turn on and grinned. Grabbing a condom, he headed into the bathroom. Water streamed over Theresa's exquisite form, plastering her hair to her slender body. He stepped around the glass bricks into the tiled enclosure already filling with steam. "Good morning, gorgeous."

She smiled and stood on tiptoes to reach his shampoo, sniffing it before putting some in her palm.

He sauntered closer and held out his empty palm. "May I?"

Her eyes focused on his other hand. "I just want to wash my hair."

He set the condom on the built-in shelf that held bottles of shampoo, conditioner, and body wash. She wiped her hand across her head, leaving a thick trail of shampoo. Richard massaged it into her scalp and through the long strands, reveling in her hair's softness, until she stepped back under the water. He filled one palm with his unscented body wash, and used two fingers of his other hand to slowly stroke it over her. She moved out of the water and leaned her head back to rinse her hair, pushing her tits upward. Unable to resist, he planted a kiss on each hardened nipple before rubbing soap onto her skin. By the time he lathered her legs, she was panting and he could smell her renewed arousal.

Pulling the shower head from the wall, he rinsed her off then changed the setting to power massage and aimed it between her legs. She gasped, a sound he was beginning to really enjoy, and her eyes rolled back into her head. Bracing her back against the tiles, she widened her stance. He played the pulsing stream over her clit until she shuddered and cried out. After propping her in the corner, he quickly washed himself off and reached for the condom packet.

"Can we skip this? I'm clean and cut." His decision to have a vasectomy had resulted in Ellen's determination to leave, but now, desperate to feel the embrace of Theresa's wet pussy on his skin, any residual regrets disappeared.

She nodded and Richard lifted her up high enough so she could slide down on his cock. He moaned and wrapped his arms around her back, leaned over, and kissed her. She slipped her arms around his neck and linked her ankles behind his back. Her lips trembled and her wonderful warm cunt clenched around his cock. Thrusting his hips, he glided in and out of her succulent sheath, driving her to another orgasm before letting himself go with a groan.

When he softened and slid out, he set her on her feet and rinsed them both off before turning off the taps and reaching for a bath towel. His stomach grumbled again.

"Maybe we should get dressed and go somewhere for breakfast?"

He rubbed her hair dry with the towel and laughed. "In Portland? On a Saturday? You want to eat breakfast or lunch?" He patted her skin dry then used it to rub himself down. "I can have an omelette made and eaten before we would get seated anywhere decent."

"You cook?"

Pulling a terrycloth robe from the linen closet, he handed it to her and grabbed his own robe off the back of the door. "I'm no chef, but I manage not to starve." Running a comb through his shoulder length hair, he pulled it back into a tight tail and straightened his bangs. He kept his hair short enough in front so he could, when necessary, tuck the tail under a hat. But her fingers through its length last night made him glad he hadn't cut the rest off.

Richard went downstairs, leaving Theresa combing through the tangles in hair that reached her tiny waist. By the time she wandered into the kitchen, he had sauteed some mushrooms, set the eggs, and was sprinkling sharp cheddar across the top before folding the omelette, dividing it into two portions, and sliding it onto to plates. He added a piece of buttered rye toast to each.

Theresa took advantage of the stepstool he had set at the end of the counter and used it to crawl up onto one of the barstools. He placed one plate in front of her and filled two mugs with coffee.

She inhaled deeply. "Smells divine."

"How do you take your coffee?"

"Milk and artificial sweetener."

He retrieved a carton of milk from the fridge and rummaged around in the pantry until he found some packets of stevia. She rewarded him with the dazzling smile that before last night had been reserved for anyone but him. Grinning back, he sat down next to her and devoured his half of the omelette wishing he had made a bigger one. Theresa pushed her plate toward him after eating only a third of the eggs and half the toast. "You still look hungry and there's way too much food here for me."

"You sure?"

She nodded and sipped at her second cup of coffee.

Well, she is tiny. Richard finished her breakfast and poured a second cup for himself. "I was serious about what I said last night."

She tilted her head, her beautiful hair framing her face, her pale skin radiant in the sunshine filtering through the skylight. "Sex isn't everything."

"I know." He sighed. "Look, I'll be perfectly honest. I hoped that you were just forbidden fruit and if we had sex I'd lose interest because I know you will never submit to me." He picked up her hand and kissed her fingers, one by one. "But, the more time I spend with you the more intrigued I become, the more," he closed his eyes and cringed before the word, the truth, left his mouth "infatuated."

She laughed and he wanted to scoop her up and carry her back upstairs. "Infatuated enough to submit to *me*?"

He raised one eyebrow above the other then lowered it when he realized that he had put on his *Master isn't pleased* face. "Look, I promise never to insult you by asking you to serve me if you'll return the favor. I'm willing to put the energy into figuring out how to make a relationship with you work, but we both must respect that line."

A frown briefly appeared and her chin stuck out in a pout that just as quickly disappeared. "Problem is, you're much more convinced than I that we should be in a," She pulled down two fingers into air quotes, "relationship. I just like the sex."

Well that's a start, at least. "But, I can try to convince you otherwise?"

She shrugged her shoulders. "I guess. I still can't figure out why that's so important to you."

Richard collected the dirty dishes and set them in the sink. "Because I'm not a friends-with-benefits kind of guy. If I'm sexually involved with a woman, I'm involved with that woman. Which doesn't mean I require exclusivity, as I said last night, I'm not monogamous and don't expect you to be. If we were in a relationship, I would just want to know about any other partners and, whenever possible share them." He winked and watched a shiver of what he hoped was desire surge through her. The thought of having him fuck a boy licking her pussy had really turned her on. That was her weakness.

"You going to the party next weekend?" He held up the coffee pot and when she shook her head put the milk back in the fridge. "Most of my current male play partners are gay, but I'm sure you have no problem finding toys to play with."

She shook her head. "Hate playing in public. Hate parties."

He tilted his head. "Why?"

"Too many lookie lous. Too many asshole Doms who hit on me thinking they can be the one to make me kneel," she looked accusingly into his eyes, "or accusing me of being a pro. Too many newbie idiots who don't know enough to stay out of range of a whip."

"If we went to a party together, no Dom would hit on you. Would you enjoy playing in public if someone protected your scene and kept the lookie loos and newbies out of your way?"

She stared at him. "Go together? Tell me, how would you feel if people assumed you were in service to me?"

He shrugged. "Wouldn't bother me, why?"

"Of course it wouldn't bother you. Because if we're seen as a couple, the assumption will be that you're the one Dom who could get me to kneel."

Richard put two fingers up to his lips, his thumb under her chin. She had a point. Of all the Dom/Domme couples he knew, the woman wore the man's collar. They might share a toy or she might have a plaything for herself, but there was a fair amount of status in owning a FemDom. "Look, I'm not saying there isn't a shitload of sex appeal in having a dominant woman in submission..."

Before he could finish his statement, she slid off the barstool and stomped toward the stairs. He strode after her. "But, that's not my goal here. I have too much respect for you and I very much understand that you're not a switch and that will never happen."

She stopped three steps up, her hand on the bannister.

"Maybe I find you so intriguing because you're possibly the only woman I know well who is as dominant as I am. And, you're only too right about other people's assumptions."

She turned halfway around and looked at him over her shoulder through a curtain of hair.

"Look, I'll never submit to you to either, but if you want to imply in public that I have, I'll not refute you. I really don't give a shit what anyone else thinks of me. As a dominant male, I don't have to prove myself. But, I know that as a Fem-

Dom you do and I understand your hostility under the circumstances."

She turned so she faced him, her arms crossed under her breasts, the terry cloth road gaping around her tiny body. He moved onto the first step so they could look each other in the eye. "I don't want your submission anymore than I wish to give you mine. I would like to have an equitable relationship with you, man to woman, woman to man. No more, no less. We can look for a submissive to share or we can each have our own, however that plays out." He held out his hands palms up.

She kept hers tucked under her arms. "Why are you so determined to go to parties with me?"

He laughed. "I adore watching you play."

She tilted her head.

"If the reasons you gave me are the only ones that prevent you from enjoying public play ..."

She put her tiny hands on his palms. If you're going to the munch this week, you could buy me a ticket."

R

When he picked her up for the party, Theresa wore a v-necked black camisole that revealed only a hint of pretty tits, a short black satiny skirt that showed off her legs, and black leather boots that came up to her knees and laced up the back. She let him help her on with a black bomber jacket and he was ready to skip the party and take her back to his place. Instead, he lifted her hair over the jacket and leaned down to kiss the back of her neck. "I hope you'll come home with me after the party, I haven't seen you for three days."

"If I do find someone I enjoy playing with, I'll probably be horny as hell."

He picked up the leather duffle that she used for a toy bag. "In that case, I'll make sure you find someone to play with." They encountered several of her neighbors in the hallways and elevator, at least one of whom gave Richard the once over. Outside, he put the duffle in the trunk with his own case, opened the passenger door for her, then settled behind the wheel.

"What type of boys do you enjoy beating?" He maneuvered out into the rain slicked street, wary as always of Portland pedestrians who routinely ignored traffic signals and crosswalks.

"Tall, slender, younger. I prefer long hair I can pull and large cocks I can torture. Other than that, it depends more on personality than looks."

"Well our tastes are similar, that's helpful. I know a lot of FemDoms like sissy boys, is that a preference?"

He saw her shrug out of the corner of his eye. "I'm not partial to sissy boys. I've no interest in forced feminization and I prefer my boys naked at home or play. But if they want to wear women's clothing at other times, I don't really care one way or the other."

He laughed. "Not big on sissies myself. But, like you said earlier, I think we need to concentrate more on personality than looks."

She shook her head. "You're really determined to find someone we both like?"

"Why not? I still believe we'd make a great team and finding a boy we could share would ..." Richard cursed under his breath as a bicyclist crossed in front of him, against the green. He concentrated on driving until they reached their destination.

By the time they filled out the consent paperwork, checked their coats, and secured their toy bags, the party was in full swing. Richard scanned those not playing, looking for someone he thought might appeal to Theresa. Several people asked if he was available to play, but he was reluctant to take them up on their offers no matter how enticing. His best bet for getting Theresa to go home with him was to find her someone to play with, and if he left her to play by herself she wouldn't enjoy her scene. Finally he spotted the only one of his regular play partners he knew was bisexual.

"Jimmy?" The lanky boy watched his Mistress flogging a busty blonde Richard had played with a few times himself.

The boy turned and dropped to his knees. "Good evening, Sir. How may I assist you?"

"Are you free to play this evening?"

"I'm always allowed to play with you at parties, Sir." Jimmy flipped his long brown pony tail over his shoulder. "What did you have in mind?"

Richard shook his head. "I was hoping you might be available to play with a friend of mine, a woman."

"May I ask who, Sir?"

Richard nodded toward Theresa who was watching a needle play session. "The Lady Theresa."

Jimmy licked his lips and his dark eyes lit up. "I've never played with her before, I would have to ask Mistress for permission when she finishes with Doreen. May I come find you if she says yes?"

"Of course, boy." Richard patted him on the head. He scanned the room again, but then saw another Dom sidling up to Theresa. He strode to her side, bent down and whispered in her ear. "You like needles?" The other Dom look startled, but he backed off.

Theresa nodded.

Richard kissed her hand and noticed a boy watching them. His mouth drooped when he saw Richard touch Theresa. "Be right back," he whispered.

He followed the boy who had wandered off to watch another scene. He wore only a black g-string revealing a gorgeous ass, plump globes just begging for a lash. "Excuse me boy, are you owned?"

The boy backed away from Richard, but he shook his head.

"Would you like to play with that lovely lady?" Richard nodded toward Theresa.

The boys blue eyes widened and the corners of his mouth turned up. "Does she... is she ... will...?"

"I'll take that as a yes. Come with me, let's see if she finds you acceptable."

"Oh, thank you, Sir. She's so beautiful."

That she is boy, that she is. The boy followed Richard back to Theresa and stood waiting while Richard whispered in her ear again. "I believe I've found someone you might enjoy playing with."

When she turned toward him, the boy fell to his knees and bowed his head.

Theresa stood up on tiptoe so she could reach Richard's ear. "He's adorable. What does he like?"

Richard shrugged. "I figured the two of you can negotiate your scene. Tonight, I'm just here to run interference."

She chuckled. "And find me pretty toys."

"That too."

Theresa stepped up to the kneeling boy. "What's your name, boy?"

"Peter, Ma'am. Thank you Ma'am."

"What do you enjoy?"

"Ma'am, if you were to find me worthy of playtime I would be willing to do anything that didn't involve blood or permanent marks."

Theresa grinned and a fire lit up her eyes. Richard had to clench one fist to maintain his own control. When she looked like that, he wanted to scoop her up and find someplace, anyplace they could fuck.

Theresa scanned the dungeon and spotted an empty cross. She pointed. "Go claim that for me, boy. I'll be there in a few minutes."

"Go ahead," Richard said. "I'll get your toy bag." By the time he found them at the cross, they apparently had completed negotiations, because she immediately extracted her cuffs and put them on the boy's wrists.

She looked up at him, her head tilted to one side. "I'm

going to do a single tail scene and I will hold you to your promise."

He grinned and nodded. "This cross doesn't have a winch, would you like me to hook him up?"

Her smile lit up her face.

"Peter, I'm just going to attach your cuffs for the lady."

"Thank you, Sir."

The boy flinched when Richard touched him and Richard suppressed a sigh. *Straight and homophobic.*

Richard stepped back. Theresa pulled her hair away from her face and swung her signal whip, just kissing the boy's pretty ass with the cracker. Peter looked over his shoulder as if to assure himself that Theresa wielded the whip and Richard had to put his arm in front of an idiot who almost crossed in front of Theresa's back swing.

By the time the boy's back was crisscrossed with red marks, Richard had steered half a dozen morons around Theresa's scene. He even went so far to ask a couple who had been loudly gossiping to take it to the social area. *No wonder she hates playing in public. Are people always this rude to FemDoms?*

When Theresa asked him to unclip the boy's cuffs, her face was flushed and her lips parted. He took her whip and squatted down to put it into the toy bag, inhaling deeply to enjoy the scent of her arousal. *Definitely worth it.*

While she gave Peter aftercare, Jimmy found him.

"Sir, my Lady would like to know why you're finding play partners for Lady Theresa and asks that you share that with her before either of you leave tonight. However, she did give me permission to do a scene with the Lady."

Richard raised one eyebrow over the other. "Is the one conditional upon the other?"

Jimmy's lower lip trembled. "I don't believe so, Sir."

"Then you will have to let Serena know that the answer to that question is private."

"May I check with Mistress, Sir?"

Richard nodded and scanned the room for an open play station. When he spotted a couple leaving another cross, he carried Theresa's toy bag over to it and waited there for Jimmy.

"Mistress is not pleased with you, Sir, but she said she will not deprive me because of your parsimony."

Knowing the word was not one Jimmy would use, Richard couldn't help laugh. "Stay here and hold the cross. I'll go let the Lady Theresa know you're available." He found her sitting on a chair in the social area, Peter kneeling at her feet, his head on her knee.

Richard sat down next to her and cringed remembering the first time he had done just that. He whispered in her ear, "I've found another toy for you to enjoy if you're interested."

To his surprise, the look she gave him could not be mistaken for anything but gratitude. "Thank you for the scene boy, but you'll have to excuse me I have another play date."

He stared at her like a rabbit begging a fox to eat it. "Will you consider my offer?"

She shook her head. "Sorry, not looking for a straight boy, right now."

Richard suppressed a grin. He knew better than to hope she was taking his interest in discovering someone for them both seriously. He guessed she just found young Peter less appealing as a potential submissive than as a toy to mark. He gave the boy a stern look that sent him scurrying for the refreshment table. Rising, he offered Theresa a hand which she took and he pulled her to her feet.

"Where?"

He bowed his head slightly. "This way."

Jimmy also requested single tail and watching Theresa play Richard understood why. He considered himself accomplished with a whip and her skill impressed *him*. Of course, they both had the same teacher. Many considered Angelo to be the most talented man with a whip on the west coast.

By the time Theresa sent Jimmy back to his Mistress, Richard didn't need to bend down to inhale her arousal. Every single male in the place, Dom and sub, seemed to be gravitating in her direction. "Shall we?"

She nodded and followed him to the coat check. He helped her on with her jacket and resisted the urge to lick her neck. Retrieving his unused toy bag, he escorted her back to his car.

Much to his delight on the way home she ran her fingers up and down his inner thigh, always drifting away before she made contact with his hardening cock.

"I take it you enjoyed yourself."

"Very much. I can't remember the last time I had so much fun at a play party, thank you."

As soon as he closed the front door of his house behind them, Theresa wrapped her arms around his waist and one leg around his thigh, grinding herself against his leg while unbuttoning his shirt.

Totally worth not getting to play tonight.

They left a trail of clothing up the stairs and by the time they reached the top, he was naked and she only had on her thigh highs and boots. He scooped her up into his arms and carried her into the bedroom. When he set her on the bed, much to his delight, she turned over and got on her hands and knees, her ass invitingly up in the air.

He growled and plunged his rock hard cock into her sopping wet cunt. "Been studying up on vanilla positions?"

She pushed back into his trust and nodded in between panting.

Richard reached around and cupped her breasts in his palms, jamming his pubes up against her pretty ass over and over again. She moaned and he released one tit so he could finger her clit until she clenched around him and every muscle in her body trembled. With a roar, he shot his load into her as she collapsed face first into the bed. He fell on his side next to her and pulled her into his arms. She fell asleep with her head on his bicep, her still booted feet hanging off the bed.

R

Theresa sat cross legged on his leather sofa, a notebook computer propped against her knees. She'd gotten in the habit of spending most of her weekends with him, but now she brought along a computer and always checked her email once or twice a day. Sometimes, if she was on deadline, she would even put time in on a project while he read or worked on his own computer. Even then, he enjoyed her company and wished he could convince her to move in permanently.

He looked up from his book when he heard a snivel and saw a single tear glistening on her cheek. Her whole face had turned down, her eyes watering, her shoulders sagging.

"What's going on?" He put down his book, set her notebook aside, and gathered her into his arms. "What's wrong?"

She pointed at the open email on her computer screen and let her head rest on his shoulder. Richard ran his fingers through her long, silky hair with one hand and retrieved the computer with the other.

"Geez, they tell you on a Saturday? By email? How long have you worked for them?"

She swallowed. "Nine years." Her voice broke.

He put the computer back down and wrapped both arms around her. "Even dominants are allowed to cry when they get kicked in the guts."

Her body didn't shake and she didn't sob, but his tee shirt got wetter and wetter from her tears. He pulled open the drawer of the table next to the sofa and extracted a box of tissues. Sitting up on his lap, she dabbed her eyes with one and blew her nose with another.

"I know it's not much consolation, but you did get severance. Have you ever thought about starting your own business?"

"I'd need at least twice the amount they're paying before I'd feel comfortable trying that."

"What if you sold or rented out your condo and moved in here?"

She raised one eyebrow over the other, a look he was sure put her toys on their knees but which he just found endearing.

"Yeah, I'm perfectly willing to take advantage of the situation if it gets you here full time."

She shrugged. "Both of us working from home? We'd drive each other bonkers."

He shook her head. "Come on, this is a big house. I can consolidate my office and give you the second room for your own."

"All those files? You wouldn't have space to move."

"Force me to weed through them and get rid of the old stuff I don't need to keep any more."

"Now's not the best time to sell."

"But, the rental market is tight. That would give you a monthly income. You'd have no living expenses. And you can invest your entire severance package into your business."

She folded her arms under her breasts, giving them definition under the voluminous white blouse she wore. "You'd do just about anything to get me to move in here, wouldn't you?"

Running one finger along her soft, pale cheek, Richard nodded. "Look, Theresa, I love you. I want to make a life with you. You keep fighting me mostly, I think, because you're worried people will think you've finally submitted."

"I've gotten over that. You've pretty much convinced everyone that I haven't and the ones who believe that I have are the same asshats who always thought they could be the one to make me kneel." She ran her fingers from her forehead back to her neck, pulling away the hairs that had strayed onto her face.

"You don't love me?" Richard cringed at the thought, the only argument he couldn't overcome, the one that would hurt more than he could bear.

"I do, that's the problem."

"Exactly why is that a problem?" He couldn't help grinning.

"Because part of what I love about you is your dominance and I can't reconcile that with my own self image."

He laughed, shaking so hard she had to grab onto his arms to keep from sliding off his lap. "Silly, don't you realize that's part of what I love about *you*? Your strength, your dominance, your ability to put some men on their knees with just a look."

"I've seen you do the same."

"And women. But that's not the point. Both of us respect each other and neither of us needs to dominate the other. The only difference is size and you must admit you enjoy the privileges mine delivers in terms of keeping pests away." He picked up her tiny hand and kissed her fingers. "And I find your diminutive size adorably sexy."

She leaned into him again, nuzzling under his chin.

"Think about it?"

She nodded, the movement rubbing her nose up and down his neck. He unbuttoned her shirt and dragged a finger along the top of her bra making his jeans uncomfortably tight. She chuckled and wiggled her hips turning uncomfortable into almost painful.

Richard set her down next to him, stood up and stripped. She unhooked her bra and let it fall open with her blouse, exposing small pale mounds and areola the color of café au lait. Richard could smell her heat. He tucked one finger on either side of her hips underneath the elastic of her track pants and dragged them and her panties down to her ankles. She kicked free of the clothing and put her feet on either side of his waist hooking her toes behind his back, pulling him toward her.

Dropping to his knees, he plunged into her and she arched her back, pushing her tight wetness further up on his cock. He caressed her breasts as he moved his hips, thrusting in and out of her. She moaned and her eyes rolled back in her head. With one hand trailing from her breast to her cunt, he kept driving into her, his balls slapping at her ass, the tip of his cock bumping up against her cervix.

When he planted his thumb on her clit, her entire body reverberated starting from her pussy clenching and unclenching against his throbbing cock, and moving outwards until her feet dropped to the floor and her arms fell to the sofa. He continued his onslaught until he made her come twice more, then let himself go and exploded inside her.

When they both stopped twitching and he slid out, Richard enveloped her with his arms and joined her on the sofa. "Well, I guess you've found one way to put me on my knees."

Theresa giggled and snuggled closer.

R

Richard entered all the data and sighed when he saw the final number. Even with all he had already paid in estimated quarterlies this past year, he'd still have a sizeable bill come next April. He needed to increase his January payment to avoid penalties. On the other hand his business had earned more this past year than the previous two. Really not something to complain about.

Looking up, he watched Theresa typing away in her office across from his own. Once she had settled in, he had rearranged his own workspace so he could watch her through the doors figuring she could always close hers if she chose. She rarely did.

That gave him an idea. He copied his tax return into a new file then made a few adjustments. Then he set up a new one and made some guesses. After arranging them so the end results of all three could all be seen on the screen, he whistled. Theresa looked up.

"Got a minute? I want to show you something."

She lifted one finger toward him, typed for a few more minutes then walked over to him and studied his screen.

"Obviously your numbers are just guesses on my part, but you can still see how much we'd save."

"You want to get married?"

"Honestly, I don't care about marriage." He put an arm around her waist and pulled her close. "I have what I want, you in my heart, my house, my bed."

She gave him a withering look.

"Well, our home and bed." He tapped the screen. "But we could save a ton."

"You want to get married this year?" She glanced up at the calendar. "In the next three weeks?"

"Why not? We could have a hell of a New Year's Eve party and neither of us would ever forget our anniversary. For that matter, we don't even have to tell folks why they're invited. Just throw a party and let them figure it out when we start the ceremony."

She laughed. "No gift registry, no presents to return, no awkward conversations before hand. Sounds perfect. I guess money wins out." She backed up to his desk, put her hands on it, and boosted herself up so she sat next to his computer. "Who shall we invite?"

"I don't care about anyone else, but Angelo has to be there."

"Absolutely."

RRR

Searching

By I. G Frederick

"We could try putting a profile up on one of those online sites?"

Theresa scowled. "That's just ludicrous. I can't tell you how much time I wasted on that crap before I met you and I never connected with anyone worthy of a second date."

Richard shrugged.

"And we would never have met online."

He laughed. "True, neither of us would have given another dominant the time of day." He opened his arms and she settled in his lap, resting her cheek against the bristly hairs of his muscular chest. He kissed her brow and dragged his fingers through her waist-length, light brown hair. "But, I couldn't imagine my life without you. We just need to find a third before one of us takes the other's head off."

Theresa sighed. "We've attended every event within driving distance including half a dozen different Munch groups. Where are we going to meet this elusive addition to our family?"

"You always see the negatives. Why not look at the positive — at least we find the same things attractive in a submissive. Imagine how much more difficult our search would be if we were both straight?"

She granted him half a nod.

"Let's go to the coast this weekend and we can relax, just the two of us, and get into the mood for Leather and Chains."

Theresa gave her husband a big grin. She already had two play dates lined up for the upcoming three-day event and hoped to find some of the other toys she enjoyed available for her amusement during the dungeon parties. "Okay. You're right, I really do need to hurt someone, but I wouldn't mind some time away with you, first."

Richard grabbed his cell from the table next to his big leather recliner and found the number for the Beach House in his contacts. "Lisa? Hi, it's Richard Stempson. Listen, I know it's short notice but I was wondering if you could find a room for me and my lovely bride for tonight and tomorrow night?"

He paused for several minutes and frowned. "I see. Can he cook?" He tilted his head. "Twenty percent off? It's a deal. I hope you have a wonderful visit to Seattle." He disconnected the call. "Lisa and Jennifer are leaving for a weekend in the Emerald City in a couple of hours. They had planned on closing down since it's still offseason. But, apparently Jennifer's nephew, who's a student at Oregon Culinary Institute, is house sitting and since we're regulars, she said she'd let us have the Rose Room at a discount." He nuzzled her neck. "We'll be the only guests."

She let her head fall back so he could kiss his way up her throat to her chin. "Sounds perfect, but I've got to get some work done first." Richard dragged his tongue along her jaw line and Theresa moaned. He pulled the strap of her bra from her shoulder.

Theresa was panting, but practicality overcame desire. "I need at least four hours on the computer before I leave the house. If you want to head out early enough to avoid rush hour ..."

Richard pressed his lips against hers then released her and guided her to her feet. "Why don't you get to it and I'll pack."

"Deal." Theresa pulled on jeans and a sweater and headed upstairs to her office.

ꟹ

When she shut down her computer at two-thirty, she found Richard had loaded the car and was waiting for her in the front room. "Looks like it'll be cool and foggy today, sunny and quite a bit warmer tomorrow. You might want to grab a jacket."

When Theresa joined him in the front seat of the Acura, he squeezed her thigh before backing out of the garage and hitting the remote to close the door. "I made six o'clock reservations at the Bite. That should give us time to check in and meet the nephew."

"As long as we don't get caught in traffic."

"Pessimist."

By the time he merged the car onto Highway 26, the rhythm of the windshield wipers and hum of the freeway beneath the car tires made it hard for Theresa to keep her eyes open.

"Take a nap, babe."

When she opened her eyes, Richard was turning from Highway 6 onto Highway 101. "Wanna stop in Tillamook?"

"No, if we drive straight through, we'll get to see the sunset."

Richard laughed and waved his left hand. "Given the clouds on the horizon, I'm guessing by the time we get to the coast all we'll see is fog, but we'll give it a shot."

When they rolled into Rockaway Beach, fog blanketed the road and Richard almost missed their turn. By the time he'd parked the car and extracted two overnight bags from the trunk, blackness engulfed them, and they cautiously climbed the steps up the hill to the house. The doorbell peeled through empty rooms. Only after Richard rapped the lion door knocker loud enough to startle the neighbor's dog into barking did a light turn on in the kitchen.

A tall, slender young man with curly brown hair opened the door and stepped aside to admit them. "Sorry, I guess I fell asleep studying. I'm Jesse." He stuck out his hand and Richard set down one of the cases to shake it.

"Richard and my wife, Theresa."

The boy's eyes widened as he stared at her and a puppy dog expression replaced the smile on his face. He had soulful brown eyes and a day's stubble on his chin.

Richard picked up the second case. "We know our way, don't trouble yourself."

"Oh, dear, I'm so sorry. You're just so beautiful." Without ever taking his eyes off Theresa, he reached out for the suitcases. "Please, let me take those up for you."

Richard shrugged and handed them over.

Jesse scurried over to the stairs, but then turned at the bottom and bowed. "After you, Ma'am, Sir."

Theresa gifted him with a smile, put her hand on Richard's arm, and walked with him up the wide, curved staircase. Jesse followed with the suitcases and set them on the luggage racks next to the fireplace in the Rose room. "Would you like me to turn this on for you?"

"Thanks, son, but we're going to go out for dinner first."

"Yes, Sir. Then I guess I'll see you in the morning. What time would you like breakfast?"

Richard laughed. "Your aunt doesn't usually give us a choice."

"I know, but since you're the only guests..."

"Then, why don't you serve at ten so we have time to take a walk on the beach before it gets crowded."

"My pleasure. I'll have the coffee on at eight, though, so you can have a cup before you head out, it you'd like."

After dinner, Theresa curled up on the plush pink love seat in front of the gas fireplace. Richard flipped the switch and squeezed in besides her. He stretched his long legs out toward the heat and wrapped his arms around her. "That boy seems rather smitten with you."

Theresa shook her head. "He's just a kid."

"I'll bet he's at least twenty-five."

"So?"

"Don't you think he's cute?"

"Yes, but he's probably Vanilla."

"I'd put money against 'nilla, too."

She shook her head. "I'm sure you'll find out more tomorrow. Right now, though, I thought we could pick up where we left off this morning."

Richard growled and ran his tongue along her chin. "Here, I believe?"

She moaned and let him push her sweater up over her breasts. He licked the skin above the lace of her bra, then unhooked the clasp to release her small, firm tits into his waiting palms. She sighed as he massaged them and licked between his fingers. Wiggling out of her sweater, she tossed it and her bra toward the chair on the other side of the bed. Richard teased one nipple with the point of his tongue and ran a hand down her back, stroking her fire-warmed skin.

Theresa unbuttoned his shirt and pushed it back over his shoulders so she could run her hands through the thick black hair on his chest and tweak his nipples with her thumbs, causing him to inhale sharply. He scooped her up in his arms and carried her to the bed, laying her across it and stretching out next to her. With his mouth attached to one nipple, he unbuttoned and unzipped her jeans, pushing them down over her slender hips. His fingers found their way between her thighs and nudged apart the silky dark curls covering her lips, seeking the moist heat within. She gasped, pushing up into his hand.

Chuckling, he stripped out of his own jeans and positioned

his hips between her legs. She wrapped her ankles around his waist, pulling him into her, relishing the piston-like strokes, the pressure his pubic bone exerted on her clit, the weight of his chest flattening her breasts.

He had one large hand on either side of her face and his tongue thrust between her lips with the rhythm of his pelvis grinding against hers. The tension built between her legs until she exploded, shaking in his arms. He chuckled again, increasing his pace and the force of his thrusts, making her come again before he grunted and shuddered.

When they caught their breath, he shifted so he lay on his back with her in his arms, her head resting on his shoulder. "Just think how delightful it would be to have that pretty boy cleaning up after me right about now."

She shivered with delightful anticipation. "I suppose you plan to proposition him over breakfast?"

"I think you'd get further, the way he stared at you..."

"And, what if he's straight?"

"Depends on how much he's willing to accept to get his sweet face between your beautiful legs."

Theresa laughed. "You're so wicked."

"Which is why you love me."

ꟹ

Stopping in the kitchen for coffee the next morning, Theresa found the disarray a bit offputting. Jesse had pots and pans on every stove burner, pieces of a food processor strewn across the counter, flour covering every surface, and half a dozen bowls of various sizes containing a puzzling array of ingredients scattered about.

But the robust aroma of freshly ground and brewed java welcomed her and he filled two travel mugs as soon as he saw them.

"Black for me, sweetener and milk for the lady."

Jesse pulled the milk carton from the fridge along with two

more travel mugs. "My aunt said she starts breakfast with a fruit smoothie, but I made them to go in case you wanted something more than coffee ...." He set all four mugs on the breakfast bar. "Orange mango."

Theresa looked into his big brown eyes and smiled. "You sweet thing, how perfect. We'll be back in a couple of hours."

The boy twisted the bottom of his stained white apron in his hands and stared at his sneakers as she followed Richard out the front door, a metal mug in each hand.

Fog muted the colors of the surrounding houses. They picked their way across the gravel road to the path leading down to the beach. Richard stuffed one of his travel mugs in his jacket pocket and took her elbow, helping her balance over the rocks the size of laundry baskets. After they jumped down from the last boulder to the packed wet sand, Theresa took a swig of the full-bodied roast. She let the heat course through her limbs before strolling toward the thundering waves. The mottled white moon still hung low in the cloud-dark sky. Gulls left claw prints in sand smooth enough to reflect the tinge of color at the edges of the clouds.

She shivered in the brisk wind and Richard wrapped one arm around her shoulder, pulling her into his warmth. They meandered north, two of only a half dozen humans visible on the beach, sipping first their coffee and then the luscious sweet combination of tropics, citrus, and yogurt. The fog burned off and the wind died down. They shed their jackets and Richard carried them over one arm. By the time she'd emptied both her mugs, her boots dangled from Richard's other hand. The sand coated her bare feet with the warmth collected from the sun, but the wind kept goose prickles raised on her skin.

Just before they turned around, Richard spotted a pile of driftwood that resembled the remains of a raft. "Perfect picture." She laughed and obligingly lounged across the boards, while he captured the pose with the beach behind her.

When they returned to the Beach House, steam covered the windows. She squealed when Richard rinsed the sand off her feet with cold water from the hose. He stomped the sand off his own boots and they let themselves into the embracing warmth and tantalizing smells. He hung their jackets, set her boots and his own on the mat under the coat rack, and padded after her in stocking feet.

The kitchen was spotless, the dishwasher humming, and a fresh pot of coffee added its aroma to that of cinnamon, onions, apples, and butter coming from the stove and oven. The large oak oval table had two place settings at one end and a platter of fruit in the center.

"Did you have a lovely walk?" Jesse had replaced his apron, shaved, and combed his hair. "I hope it wasn't too cold. More coffee?" He lifted the pot.

Richard held out Theresa's chair and she pointed to the empty mug in front of her as she settled into her seat. "Please."

After filling both her and Richard's cups, Jesse added milk and a packet of sweetener to hers then scurried back into the kitchen. He emerged moments later with a platter of steaming apple walnut muffins which he placed between them.

Theresa only had time to inhale deeply of the cinnamon laced fruit and nut scents before Jesse returned again and set plates on the quilted placemats in front of each of them. "Careful, they're hot." In the center a ramekin held eggs, cooked with bits of red pepper and mushrooms, topped with Swiss cheese. Chunks of red potatoes sautéed with onions filled half the plate and two fat, juicy sausages adorned the other side.

Theresa added a muffin to her plate and broke off a bit of the top. "Yummy," she said after the flavors invaded her mouth.

"Very nice." Richard cut off a piece of the sausage and blew on it before popping it in his mouth. "How long have you studied at the Institute?"

"I have one more term to complete my culinary arts diploma."

"And what do you plan to do when you graduate?"

"Not sure, really. I'm .. well ... I don't ..." He turned and grabbed the coffee pot. "Here, let me top you off."

Theresa dipped a spoon into the egg dish and closed her eyes to enjoy the combined flavors of sweet peppers, earthy crimini, and savory cheese. She looked up to see Jesse staring at her, his brows scrunched together, his eyes pleading. "It's lovely, boy."

His face relaxed and he grinned. "I'm glad you like it, Ma'am."

She raised one eyebrow over the other. "You've a flair for cooking, but I'm wondering if you have any other talents?" She nibbled on a chunk of potato.

He trembled, the coffee in the pot coming dangerously close to spilling over.

Richard cleared his throat. "Put that down before you burn yourself, boy."

"Yes, Sir." He turned and, using both hands, set the pot back on the hotplate. "I'm sorry, Sir."

Richard tilted his head and looked at Theresa. She nodded.

"Why are you apologizing, boy?"

He turned slowly, his lips pressed together so tightly they disappeared in a thin line across his pale face. "Your wife, is so beautiful, Sir," he whispered so softly Theresa had to stop chewing the succulent strawberry she'd lifted from the fruit plate to hear his words.

She laughed. "That still doesn't explain why you're apologizing." Picking up a whole sausage between two fingers, she pressed one end against her lips and slowly sucked in an inch of it while Jesse's eyes grew so wide she thought they would get stuck open. She chomped into the meat and licked the grease off her lips in slow motion.

Jesse was panting and even Richard's breath was heavy in her ear.

Chewing the sausage, she stared at Jesse's apron-covered

crotch and wondered how tight his jeans had gotten. The boy sunk to his knees so gradually, at first she didn't realize he was moving. She took a sip of coffee. "Tell me, boy, what is it you wish most of all that you could do right now?"

Jesse collapsed on himself, burying his face against his knees. "You'll laugh," he sobbed.

Theresa softened her tone. "I can't promise you anything boy, except that. There's nothing you could tell me right now that would make us laugh."

Richard mouthed the words "I told you so" at her.

"You won't tell my aunt?"

"Of course, not, boy. What business is it of hers?"

He mumbled something against his jeans.

Theresa nibbled on her muffin. "Speak up, boy, I can't hear you."

Richard scooped up a fork full of potatoes, silently forming the word "feet" before putting it in his mouth.

Jesse lifted his face up high enough to clear his mouth. "I just want to kiss your feet." He trembled. "And, maybe suck on your toes. You have such lovely, delicate feet."

"I would love to have you worship my feet, boy. But, first I want to finish enjoying this delicious breakfast you've made us. Then I can move to a more comfortable chair and you can show me what other talents you have.

Jesse bolted upright, his eyes wide, his lips parted, his breathing ragged. "Really? But, you're married."

Theresa laughed. "That doesn't mean I'm monogamous." She took one last bite of sausage and pushed her plate toward Richard who exchanged it for his empty one.

"Do you know what a FemDom is, boy?" She snagged another strawberry from the fruit platter.

Jesse's pale skin blazed red. "Yes, Ma'am. May I ask, is your husband in service to you?"

She laughed. "No, he's also a dominant. And, we're searching for a third who would be submissive to us both." Suddenly, she realized why the boy had fallen apart when asked about his career aspirations. "What other schools have you attended, boy?"

He smiled. "I've studied massage, hair and nail care, and sewing, Ma'am."

She avoided acknowledging the smug look on her husband's face.

"My family thinks I can't make up my mind and pick a career. But, I was hoping to," he cleared his throat, "find a lady who would appreciate all the skills I've acquired."

"I see." She emptied her cup and raised her hand when Jesse jumped up and reached for the pot. Richard scraped up the last of the potatoes. "Shall we adjourn to the sitting room?"

Richard nodded.

"I'll go start the fire." Jesse tore down the hallway.

Richard rose and kissed her forehead. "He's cute. Reel him in for me, will you?" He followed her into the sitting room off the main entrance. Apparently Jesse had previously laid out a fire because he already had it blazing. He pulled one of two stuffed leather armchairs up in front of it. Theresa settled into the comfy cushions and waited while Richard looked at the other chair with a raised eyebrow. Jesse finally took the hint and pulled that one so it was facing hers. Richard plopped into it, stretching his stocking feet out toward the fire, his fingers intertwined on his flat belly, a self-satisfied grin on his face.

Jesse knelt in front of Theresa and she extended her right leg in his direction. He held her heel in his palm and dragged a warm finger along first one side of her cold foot and then the other. "So soft." He leaned forward, then looked up, pleading with his eyes.

Theresa smiled and nodded. He closed his eyes, pressed his lips against the top of her foot, and moaned. He kissed his way to her big toe and licked it, the heat of his lips and tongue warming her skin. She sighed. He grinned and sucked her toe into his mouth, caressing it with his lips and tongue until she purred. The expression on Jesse's face shifted and he adjusted his position so, without removing his mouth from her toe, he could massage her heel and the ball of her foot with his thumbs. She melted under the combination of eager nuzzling and skillful massage. By the time he finished with her other foot, more than her feet were tingling. Theresa's panties were damp and her hips wiggled of their own volition.

Richard must have left the room, but she didn't notice until he strode back in and stood next to Jesse, one hand behind his back. "Smell that delectable aroma, boy?"

Jesse's blushed. "Yes, Sir."

"How badly do you want to taste it?"

"Sir?"

"You clean, boy?"

"I was tested six months ago and I've not ..." He kissed one foot and then the other. "I mean ... I'm not..."

"I take your meaning, boy." Richard's voice was husky. He wanted the boy, badly. "You still haven't answered my question."

"What do I have to do?"

"I'll let you lick my wife's pussy as long as she can stand it and your tongue holds out."

"In exchange for?"

"Your ass is mine."

Jesse shuddered. He wrapped his arms across his chest, gripping his biceps. "I've never," he whispered.

Richard ran his hair through Jesse's curls, tilted his head back, and kissed him. "I'll keep that in mind."

Theresa unbuttoned her jeans and ever so slowly lowered the zipper. Jesse sobbed.

"Well, boy, you've got my wife all hot and bothered. One of us is going to have to go muff diving. Since you've pleased her, you can watch. Or ..." he dropped a towel, a bottle of lube, and a strip of condoms in Theresa's lap.

The boy rocked back and forth, trembling.

Balancing the condoms and lube bottle on one chair arm,

Theresa stood long enough to put the towel on the seat cushion and slide her jeans and panties slowly down over her hips, her blouse dropping to cover her upper thighs. She sat back down and lifted her legs, pointing her toes at Jesse. He pulled her pants off by the legs and tossed her jeans on the chair Richard had vacated. He stared at the spot where her legs disappeared under white cotton.

She opened her knees just enough to release her scent. With a cry, Jesse dove forward, kissing the tender skin of her thighs while he untied his apron and unzipped his jeans. He inhaled deeply and Theresa threw one leg over the empty chair arm to give him better access. Richard's pants fell to the floor with a clunk of keys and wallet. He grabbed the condoms and lube as he stepped out of them. Jesse stuck out his tongue and ran it the length of her slit. Theresa sighed and slid lower in the chair.

Richard lifted Jesse's head by his hair long enough to pull the apron strap off his neck. When he released the boy's hair, Jesse dove back in. He thrust the point of his tongue into her and nuzzled her clit with his nose. Richard unbuttoned Jesse's shirt, removed it, then pulled away his jeans. Theresa enjoyed the view of the boy's firm ass sticking up in the air and Richard's sheathed cock pointing at her while Jesse nibbled on her nub with his lips. Overwhelmed with sensory stimulation, Theresa shuddered, her come gushing out over his face.

"Oh, yum," he muttered and licked and sucked and licked.

Richard knelt behind him, pouring lube into his hand. He slathered it over his rod and then shoved a lubed finger into Jesse's ass. The boy moaned and Theresa came again. By the time Richard had three fingers in the boy, he was squirming but he never stopped licking and sucking. She draped her legs over his naked shoulders and he pushed in so deeply, she worried he couldn't breathe. But his chest expanded and contracted in rapid gasps and his cock pointed down, straight and hard. Although not as thick as Richard, his dick was longer and Theresa thought he would make a lovely CBT toy.

Spreading the boy's cheeks, Richard eased himself into his ass, pushing until his pubes were up against the boy's skin. Jesse groaned, his breath hot against Theresa's clit. Richard slid back then pushed forward again. He moved slowly at first, but gradually he increased his speed until he slammed against the boy's ass. He leaned forward and reached around the boy, grabbing his nipples in between his thumb and forefinger. Jesse cried out, the vibrations sending Theresa off into another paroxysm. The boy shook and spurted all over the polished wood of the floor. Richard grunted and paused deep inside Jesse's ass.

When Richard eased out, Jesse sat back on his heels, his face in his hands, his shoulders shaking.

Theresa leaned forward and pulled him into her arms. He rested his cheek against her chest, his tears wetting her blouse.

Richard stripped off the condom. "I'll let it go this once, but next time you'd better get permission before you come, boy."

Jesse blinked. "Next time? Sir?" He looked up into Theresa's eyes and she smiled at him.

"We're looking for more than a sex toy, boy." Richard wiped his hands on the edge of the towel hanging from the chair. "And you've expressed a willingness to make yourself useful in a number of ways we find very attractive. If you're interested, we'd like to take you home and try you out."

Jesse hiccuped. "Yes, Sir, thank you Sir."

Theresa stroked his curls. "Why were you crying, boy?"

Without lifting his head from her chest, he wiped a finger under each eye. "I've never thought of myself as queer before."

"You may not be. Do you find Richard attractive?"

He shrugged. "Not really. I mean he's good looking, no offense, Sir. But, I think I'm straight."

"No offense taken, boy. Your orientation isn't really important, as long as you're willing to serve us both."

The boy nuzzled against Theresa, but didn't respond. His breathing slowed to normal before he spoke. "I think you've figured me out, already, Sir. I want to serve the Lady and I'll do anything to earn that privilege, even if that includes having sex with you. Is that acceptable?"

Richard laughed. "It's more than acceptable, boy, it's hot."

Jesse pushed himself up on the arms of the chair. "May I go get a rag to clean up my mess, Sir."

"Yes, boy, and bring us both some more coffee."

"Yes, Sir."

Jesse returned with a worn towel draped over his arm, carrying a silver tray. When they took their cups from the tray, he set it on a table, and wiped up the floor with the towel.

"May I ask what your plans are for the rest of the day? Will you be eating out or would you like me go shopping so I can make dinner."

Richard smiled. "We'll eat here, but I think the first order of business is to spend some time discussing our expectations and your hopes."

"Yes, Sir. May I clear the breakfast dishes first?"

"Go ahead."

Jesse staggered out of the room and Richard plopped back into his chair. "Guess you were right about online."

She snickered. "I suppose you anticipated something like this?"

He shook his head. "No expectations. Just the ability to recognize and the willingness to take advantage of whatever opportunity presents itself."

ꟹ

After three hours of questions and negotiations, Richard settled down with his tablet to draft a six-month contract, Jesse headed for the grocery store, and Theresa luxuriated in silky, rose scented, steaming hot water. When the water turned cold, she emerged to the aroma of garlic, onions, and wine wafting through the house. She found a black, spandex, halter dress Richard had packed hanging in the closet and slipped into it, skipping underwear. Rummaging in her overnight bag, she found Richard also had packed a pair of black, patent leather shoes with three-inch spike heels. She put them on and went downstairs.

Richard, a glass of wine in his hand, leaned against the counter, watching Jesse scurry about the kitchen. When he saw her, he lifted his free arm. She stepped near and he pulled her against his shoulder, running his hand down her back to caress her ass through the thin fabric of the dress.

"I was just telling the boy that I sent him the draft contract via e-mail and I want him to take his time reviewing it after we leave. If we agree on terms, he can move in with us as soon as he finishes his last two months at the Institute."

"That sounds delightful." She accepted the glass Jesse offered and inhaled the fruity bouquet. "Will school occupy all your time or will you be able to visit?"

"I'll make time, Ma'am." Jesse flipped off the stove burners and lowered the oven temperature.

After dinner, Richard went out to the car and returned with a leather duffel bag. Theresa licked her lips. Jesse stared at it with a quizzical look on his face. Slowly, his eyes widened, his mouth opened, and his lower lip trembled. Theresa nodded and he dropped the pan he held in his hands into the sink with a clatter.

"Why don't you leave the dishes until morning, boy." Richard lifted the satchel.

Jesse stared at it, turning his head from side to side. "I don't know if ... I'm not sure... I've never ..."

Theresa stepped around the counter and ran a hand along the tight denim covering Jesse's lovely, firm ass. "Don't worry, boy. I'll be gentle." She slid her hand around to his crotch and grabbed his already hardening package. "At first." She stepped in closer. In her heels, she stood tall enough to reach his neck with her lips. "You do know the definition of a sadist, don't you, boy?"

"Ssssomeone who likessss to hurt people?" He was shaking, but he leaned back and she wrapped her arms around him, pressing her breasts against his back.

"Close. Someone who gets sexually aroused from inflicting pain."

Jesse turned, dropped to his knees, and wrapped his arms around her hips. "I want to please you, Ma'am."

She ran her fingers through his silky curls. "I know boy. And that turns me on."

He inhaled deeply. "What do you want me to do?"

"Well, the first thing you need to do is get rid of these clothes. In fact, I'd rather you not wear any for the rest of our visit. At home, you'll not be permitted to wear clothing except when you leave the house."

"Yes, Ma'am." He fumbled with the buttons of his shirt, but only got two undone. Untying his apron, he lifted it off his neck, then pulled his still-buttoned shirt over his head. Hands shaking, he set them on a chair and struggled to unfasten his jeans. He had them down around his ankles before he thought to remove his shoes.

Standing with his hands over his crotch in only his socks and his blue bikini underwear, he looked at her with those puppy dog eyes.

Theresa stepped close and pushed the elastic down over his hips. "You won't need these." She ran one finger along the side of his cock, smiling when it twitched and lengthened. She tugged one of his hands away from the other and led him out of the kitchen. He stepped free of his underpants and followed her to the staircase. Richard set the duffel on the fifth stair and unzipped it. He extracted a pair of leather cuffs and handed her first one then the other so she could buckle them around Jesse's wrists.

Wrapping a towel around one of the balusters, Richard

clipped Jesse's cuffs together on the other side so he stood at the curve of the staircase with his hands bound together above his head. Richard handed Theresa a single tail and she cracked it to one side. Jesse jumped. Theresa ran her free hand along the soft skin of Jesse's ass and around to his rock hard cock. "Ready, boy?"

"I guess so, Ma'am."

Theresa stepped back far enough so she could swing the whip without touching Jesse. Slowly, she eased forward until the cracker kissed his skin. He flinched and her pussy muscles clenched. She stayed back for a dozen strokes, letting him get used to the sensation, then stepped an inch forward so the leather hit his skin hard enough to cause pain.

"Ouch, ouch, ouch, ooooohhhhhh." Jesse fell forward against the stairs and Richard reached through the balusters to steady the lad. Theresa could feel her juices trickling down the inside of her thigh.

She inched forward so the whip marked the skin on his ass and shoulders red, without raising welts. Richard held the boy's arms, keeping him from hanging from his wrists. She was breathing heavily now. Richard shook his head and Theresa let the whip fall to her side. She pressed her body against Jesse's back, crisscrossed with red marks. He moaned and she rubbed the damp fabric of her dress against his ass. The boy had sense enough to stick one leg back, allowing her to hump it, rubbing her clit against his thigh until she came with a shudder.

Richard chuckled and released his erect cock from his pants, dangling it in front of Jesse's lips. The boy obediently opened them, allowing Richard to slide inside the moist heat. Watching their new toy suck on her husband's dick turned Theresa on even more. She pulled her dress over her head, tossed it over the railing, and pressed her naked flesh against the heat of Jesse's back. The boy wiggled his ass and she raked her fingernails across the red marks from her whip.

As soon as Richard filled the boy's mouth, she unclipped

the cuffs, grabbed Jesse's hair, and pulled him to his knees. She threw one leg over his shoulder and shoved her dripping pussy into his face. Glassy eyed, the boy sucked on her nub until she gushed all over his face. Richard appeared behind her, reaching around to toy with her nipples. She took a fistful of Jesse's hair in each hand to steady herself. With a cry she came again and fell back into Richard's arms.

"Can you make it up the stairs, boy?"

"I think...I'll try."

By the time he laid her across the bed, Richard was hard again. He thrust himself inside her and she was vaguely aware of Jesse crawling into the room on all fours. While her pussy spasmed around Richard's cock, she stretched one hand out to Jesse and he knelt beside the bed, pressing his head against her palm so she could stroke his curls. When Richard finally spent himself inside her, Theresa was trembling in ecstasy. Richard stretched out beside her, one hand on her breast.

"I've made a bit of a mess, boy. Clean her up."

"Yes, Sir." Jesse worked his mouth up one thigh and down the other, sucking up the sticky combination of her cum and Richard's. Then he licked everything he could from her bush and slurped Richard's semen from her cunt. She opened her legs and Jesse's lips attached themselves to her clit, sucking on it until she exploded, her body shaking in Richard's arms.

When she finally stopped trembling, she grabbed Jesse's curls and pulled him up to lay besides her. Richard reached across her and fondled his head while Jesse clung to her, his arms wrapped around her waist. Theresa fell asleep embraced by her husband and their submissive, grateful that their search was over.

ઉઉ ઉઉ ઉઉ

Jesse

By I.G. Frederick

From his aunt's front porch, Jesse watched the robin's egg blue Acura disappear around the corner, heading toward Highway 101. Sobbing, he stepped back inside, locked the front door, and slid to the tile floor. His shoulders shook and tears streamed down his face. The marks on his butt and across his shoulders from the Lady's whip still throbbed, but those gave him only pleasant memories. He would never forget his first taste of the amazing, delicious ambrosia between her legs, her soft naked body pressed against the welts on his back.

But, he also never would be able to erase the pain in his ass from her husband pounding into it with his huge cock, the taste of the man's spunk filling his mouth and mixed with the Lady's honey.

What have I done? Jesse crawled into the kitchen and pulled himself up to the counter so he could clean up the breakfast dishes. The words of the contract he had signed tumbled through his head. For the next six months, they owned him. Both of them.

The beautiful Lady Theresa embodied everything he could have hoped for – she was the woman he had trained to serve since high school when he chose home economics over shop. He had earned certificates in massage, cosmetology, and, in another few months, culinary arts – all skills he'd hoped to use to entice a beautiful Domme to accept him as her full-time slave.

And, she had. ... But, she was married. ... And her husband ...

Jesse started the dishwasher and poured himself the last of the coffee. The Lady had kissed him goodbye on the lips before she left. He'd knelt at the door as they departed to return to Portland. But, he couldn't savor her taste on his lips because Sir Richard had followed her kiss with his own.

Was he gay, now? He'd let a man come in his mouth and his ass. Did that make him queer? Or just a whore, allowing Sir Richard to abuse him for the privilege of licking the Lady's beautiful toes, and tasting her sweet nectar?

Jesse poured the now cold coffee down the sink. His aunt and her wife would be back in a few hours and he needed to make sure no evidence remained of the past two days' activities. He thoroughly cleaned the guest room the Lady and Sir Richard had shared, where all three had slept in the king bed last night. Although his aunt had said to just leave the dirty linens in the laundry room, he washed the sheets and the towels.

Afraid the smell of semen on the stairs and in the sitting room existed outside his imagination, he cleaned the entire house except the bedroom and bathroom his aunt shared with her wife and which no one had entered.

When he could only smell lemon oil and Murphy's oil soap, he climbed into the shower of the room they let him stay in between school terms to get away from his family. As he washed off the sweat and grime from cleaning, he found his mind wandering again to the beautiful, tiny Lady Theresa. She couldn't be more than five feet tall and probably weighed less than a hundred pounds. Her small breasts were so perky and pretty, her tiny toes delicious in his mouth. And the heavenly taste of the juices that poured from the soft moist folds between her legs ... he got hard just thinking about her.

Sir Richard's words echoed in his head as he stroked his rigid cock with a soapy hand: "I'll let it go this once, but next time you'd better get permission before you come, boy." *Is that only when I'm with them?* He tried to remember if the contract included any mention of whether or when he could come when he was alone. By then it was too late and he had to rinse his jism off the tile walls of the shower stall.

He'd better read the document more carefully before he packed to return to Portland and his last term at the Culinary Institute.

The Lady lived with her husband in a beautiful house in Portland's West Hills, only a short bus ride from the school. The first time he visited, Sir Richard answered the door. Jesse tried not to let his disappointment show. As instructed in the list of protocols they had emailed him, he knelt on the slate at Sir Richard's feet and leaned over and kissed the tops of first one and then the other of the tall man's bare feet.

"Our offices are at the top of the stairs. You can come up there after you've stripped, boy."

"Yes, Sir. Thank you for the privilege of serving you, Sir."

Sir Richard patted the top of his curls and turned to go up the wide, carpeted stairway. Jesse removed his clothing, still infused with the scent of garlic and basil from the pesto made for his last class of the week, and tied the black bow tie around his neck. He hesitated before preceding up the stairs long enough to take a deep breath. Feeling like the princesses' lover, he wondered whether he would meet the lady or the tiger at the top.

He found two open doors: on the left, her back to the hallway, typing away on a computer keyboard, was the exquisite Lady Theresa. On the right, facing the hallway, seated behind a desk in the middle of the room, was the tiger, Sir Richard, lustfully watching Jesse's every move.

Jesse nodded, but since he had not yet greeted the Lady, he entered her office and dropped to his knees on the thick gray carpet, just to the right of her chair where she could see him out of the corner of her eye. After a dozen more keystrokes, she turned her chair so she faced him and extended her lovely, tiny feet in his direction. Jesse pressed his lips to her soft flesh, dragging them from her toes to her ankle on first one foot than another. He whimpered with pleasure.

She ran her fingers through his curls, then pulled his head away from her feet. He tried to suppress his reaction, but couldn't help mewling.

"Business before pleasure, boy. I have to finish this proposal. Richard will give you your assignment."

"Yes, Ma'am. May I call you Mistress, Ma'am?" Jesse clapped his hands over his mouth, wondering where the boldness to ask that question had come from.

She laughed and he drank in the delicious melody. "You may, boy." She leaned over and kissed his forehead. "But, only if you call Richard, Master."

Jesse's chin hit his chest. "Yes, Ma'am," he whispered. "I understand, Ma'am."

"Who you report to will change depending on whose deadline is more pressing, but for today, Richard's in charge of putting you to work."

"Yes, Ma'am. Thank you for the privilege of serving you, Ma'am."

Jesse crawled out of the room and knelt in the doorway of Sir Richard's office. Fortunately, he appeared to be working as well.

"Start by preparing dinner. For tonight, you'll have to make do with what's in the fridge and pantry. Tomorrow, I'll go to the Farmer's Market, a chore I expect you eventually to assume responsibility for, and you can let me know if you've any requests.

At the bottom of the staircase, Jesse seriously considered putting his clothes back on, and running for the bus stop. But, he had signed a contract. He had agreed to serve for six months with the hope that he would them be considered for a collar and a permanent position. And, as much as he hated the thought of what Sir Richard might do to him, the allure of the beautiful Lady Theresa made almost anything her husband required acceptable.

Jesse pulled a pan of biscuits out of the top oven and looked up to see Sir Richard escorting the Lady in to the dining room. Unable to move, Jesse watched as the man, who towered over his wife, kissed her neck after helping her into her seat.

"Smells good, boy. I take it you found enough to work with?"

"Yes, Sir. Thank you, Sir." Jesse eased the biscuits into a napkin lined basket and placed it on the table he had set for two. From the bottom oven, he extracted a ratatouille he had made with the vegetables left over from the previous weeks' market excursion and the pieces of chicken he had battered in flour and buttermilk before frying.

He set those on the table and filled their glasses from the open bottle of Chianti he had found in the pantry.

The Lady Theresa spooned a tiny portion of the casserole onto her plate and added a leg and one biscuit. "You didn't set a place for yourself?"

Jesse clutched the hot pads to his chest.

Sir Richard pushed the chair across from him out from the table with his feet. He filled half his plate with ratatouille then added three pieces of chicken and several biscuits. "We're not looking for a servant, boy. We want to add a member to our family."

"Yes, Sir, Ma'am." Jesse scurried to the kitchen, brought out another place setting, and stood by the chair.

"You may sit, boy."

The oak seat was cold against his bare ass. Jesse helped himself to dinner, never taking his eyes of the Lady Theresa.

She ate his chicken with a knife and fork and dipped her biscuit in the ratatouille's tomato base. "Delicious."

"That it is." Sir Richard buttered his biscuits and kept them away from the sauce.

Jesse nibbled at his food, pleased with his efforts for the most part, but noting the ratatouille could use more basil. "Thank you, Ma'am. Sir."

Sir Richard licked his fingers. "I'm surprised the school would teach you anything so pedestrian as fried chicken."

"None of this is stuff I learned in school, Sir." Jesse took a sip of wine, trying to calm his nerves. "My mom's family's from the south and the chicken is an old family recipe. He scooped up a bit of eggplant from his plate. "My dad's Italian and his mother lived with us, and did much of the cooking, when I was a child."

Sir Richard captured Jesse's eyes with his dark brown ones. "Southern? Italian? What exactly have you told your parents about where you're spending the weekend?"

Jesse swallowed and tried to lower his eyes, but couldn't escape the man's mesmerizing gaze. "I told them I was going to the coast with some friends from school."

"And next weekend?" Sir Richard scraped up the last of the tomato sauce from his plate.

"Haven't thought that far ahead, Sir." Jesse emptied his wine glass in one gulp.

"Just out of curiosity, which side of your family is your aunt related to?"

"Neither, really. Aunt Lisa was married to my father's brother for five years. I'm the only one in the family who's spoken to her since they divorced and I'm not sure my family even knows she's married to a woman, now." Jesse, pushed the remainder of his eggplant around on his plate, trying to avoid Sir Richard's scrutiny. "Aunt Lisa, and now Jennifer, have been the only adults I could talk to about," he cleared his throat, "adult subjects who I know would give me an informative answer instead of just outrage that I'd ask the question."

Richard laughed. "You don't have to use euphemisms here, boy. You can talk to Lisa and Jennifer about sex."

Jesse shook his head. "Not about sex. About service and submission."

This time the Lady Theresa laughed and Jesse felt the tips of his ear turn red. "Service and submission *are* sexual, boy. Even if there's no contact that might be considered sex." Out of the corner of his eye he saw her pull air quotes around the last word. "D/s and BDSM are still all about physical attraction and interaction."

Sir Richard finished his wine and shook his head when Jesse reached for the bottle. "How did you know you could talk to Lisa and Jennifer about BDSM?"

"Once when I was house sitting and looking for something to read, I found a copy of *The Loving Dominant* on one of their nightstands."

Richard harrumphed. "Interesting, I never would have taken them for a D/s couple."

Jesse shrugged. "They're not. They have friends, though, and they were looking at whether making the B&B kink friendly would help with occupancy."

"I take it they decided against it."

"They were afraid it wasn't worth the risk of pissing off their neighbors. Rockaway is a rather tiny town."

The Lady Theresa pushed her plate toward the center of the table. "That it is. But, enough chit chat. I was hoping to get some playtime in this evening. The boy deserves a reward for such a lovely dinner."

Jesse cringed. He didn't exactly think of a whipping as a reward. But, he remembered how horny the Lady got when she beat him. That might be worth it. *Of course, if she lets you do anything, you'll also have to put up with his cock.* Jesse sighed. "May I clean up the dishes, first, Ma'am?"

"Of course, boy. Meet us downstairs when you're done."

When Jesse crept down the carpeted stairs to the basement, he discovered an elegant room decorated in red and black and furnished with items he had only seen online – a Saint Andrew's cross, a spanking bench, a rack from which various kinds of whips hung, and shelves of other torture implements, many he couldn't identify. The Lady sat on a massage table in the middle of the room, and Sir Richard stood between her legs, holding her in his arms, kissing her.

Jesse knelt in view but as far as he could get from the table. He tried to mimic the position he had seen in pictures, his ass on his heels, his hands palm up on his naked thighs, his back straight, his chin on his chest. His cheeks grew hot when he looked down to see his cock sticking straight out.

"Oh, perfect." Sir Richard's bare feet and hairy legs filled Jesse's field of vision. He grabbed Jesse by the hair and pulled him to his feet, dragging him over to the table.

Lady Theresa patted the table and smiled when Jesse lay down on his back on the padded leather and Sir Richard cuffed his hands to the sides.

Sir Richard handed her a plastic box the size of a shoe box. "Do you know what CBT is, boy?"

Jesse swallowed. "Cock and ball torture, Sir."

Sir Richard chuckled.

The Lady set the box between Jesse's knees and one by one extracted black, plastic clothespins which she attached to his scrotum. Jesse winced.

"Don't worry, boy. It'll hurt more when she takes 'em off." Sir Richard's laugh sent a shiver up and down Jesse's spine.

When his balls bristled with clothespins and he wondered if any of his skin would survive, Lady Theresa ran her hand over the tops of them until Jesse whimpered. Then, a dozen pieces of long thin plastic hit his dick. He screamed and his eyes flew open. The Lady held a miniature flogger with six-inch long thin, knotted, tails and used it to whip his engorged cock. The pain reverberated through his entire body, exceeded only by an inexplicable and overwhelming desire to jerk off.

Sir Richard forced Jesse's head to one side and thrust his immense prick into Jesse's mouth. He had to breathe through his nose to avoid gagging. With Sir Richard shoving his pubes up against Jesse's face, he couldn't see what the Lady was doing, but he felt tiny metal teeth pricking his skin, intensifying his pain. His balls tightened and only the fear of Sir Richard's punishment should he spew spunk at the Lady kept him from losing control.

His jaw ached from Sir Richard slamming in and out of his mouth. Then the Lady started removing clothespins. Sir Richard's cock prevented Jesse's shriek from emerging as anything more than a gurgle. Sir Richard chuckled and the Lady giggled. Jesse gripped the sides of the table so tightly, his knuckles turned white. Tears spilled out of his eyes.

Sir Richard filled Jesse's mouth with his foul jism and Jesse swallowed only to avoid choking. His balls ached and his cock throbbed. The beautiful Lady Theresa had removed her clothing and she knelt on the table, one knee on either side of Jesse's face. He had no idea how or when she had climbed up there, but he lifted his head grateful to replace her husband's foul flavor with the delectable honey that dripped from her luscious folds.

Embarrassed by his amateur attempts to please the Lady at the coast, Jesse had studied every video and book he could find on cunnilingus. He was vaguely aware of Sir Richard standing next to the table, kissing and caressing his wife. Jesse tried to ignore him by concentrating on the supple flesh above his face, stroking her folds with his tongue, thrusting it as far into her as he could, nuzzling her nub with his nose.

Additional honey pouring into his mouth rewarded his efforts. When she shuddered, her juices flooded his face and he ignored the evidence that her own cries were muffled by Sir Richard's tongue in her mouth. The ache in his cock intensified until a cold, lubed finger penetrated his ass. Sir Richard lifted the Lady from his face after her third orgasm and Jesse whimpered, scrunching his eyes closed, bracing himself for another assault.

But the cock pushing into his rectum felt stiffer and even bigger than Sir Richard's. Jesse opened his eyes to find the Lady leaning over his chest, her soft breasts sliding across his skin. He lifted his head to see she wore a black leather harness that secured a large purple dildo in front of her pubes. Jesse moaned.

Sir Richard climbed up behind his wife and Jesse heard the splurging of his dick pushing in and out of the Lady, shoving her strapon cock deep into Jesse's ass. Her eyes rolled back in her head when Sir Richard reached his hands around to caress her beautiful breasts. Jesse licked his lips, wishing more than anything he could wrap them around the Lady's stiff nipple.

She moaned, her entire body shuddered, and she collapsed on Jesse, her taught belly pressing his turgid cock against his pubes. Sir Richard slammed into her twice more then roared as he emptied himself into her. Jesse wondered what would happen to him if the Lady became pregnant. Sir Richard had only worn condoms when fucking Jesse in the ass.

The Lady's soft skin pressed against Jesse's cock and he had to bite his lip to avoid having her touch send him over the edge.

Finally, Sir Richard withdrew and climbed down from the table, lifting the Lady down and setting her on her feet in front of Jesse. "I think the boy deserves a reward and I'm guessing he'd appreciate it from you more so than from me."

The Lady smiled at him and leaned over just far enough so Jesse could reach her nipple with his tongue. He moaned in delight and licked everywhere he could touch. When she lowered her lovely mound so he could finally wrap his lips around her nipple, a huge hand gripped his cock.

"You may come, boy." Sir Richard squeezed tight, but otherwise didn't move his fingers. Just the pressure was enough to send Jesse over the edge and he wept with relief as he spurted all over his own stomach.

The Lady stood upright and Jesse suppressed a whimper. "Thank you so very much, Ma'am ... Sir."

Monday afternoon on the Max ride home from school, Jesse dreaded returning to his parent's house. After three days serving the Lady, he almost couldn't bear the thought of pretending to be a normal student. He knew his parents would ask him about his weekend and he didn't have a clue what to say. He couldn't exactly tell them that it was magnificent, terrifying, delightful, painful, and exhilarating. His cock still stung and his balls still ached. He had chosen to stand for the thirty-minute ride rather than sit on his sore buttocks after the paddling Sir Richard had given him Saturday night before fucking him in the ass while the Lady sat on his face again.

By the time he walked from the Max to his parent's bungalow they had, as he'd hoped, already retired. He'd stayed late at school to get his assignments done, and scrounged leftovers for dinner. The only light in the house, besides the one in the front entry, was the thin strip that appeared under their bedroom door. Jesse let himself in, locked the front door, and crept up the stairs to his bedroom.

"Is that you, son?" his father shouted.

"Yeah, Dad. Had a lot of schoolwork. Have to get up early. See you in the morning?" Jesse ducked into his room and fell face first across his bed. But, he couldn't sleep. Instead, he booted his laptop and logged into the BDSM site the Lady had recommended. The twelve options for gender presented no problem, he simply selected male. But, he had no clue what to choose from the twelve alternatives for sexuality or the 27 for "role," so he marked both as "unsure."

He found profiles for the Lady Theresa and Sir Richard, but asking to be their "friends" seemed inappropriate, so he just sent a message to the Lady Theresa to let her know the handle he had chosen. After haunting the various forums until almost midnight, he crawled into bed still confused.

When Jesse returned home from school the next night, he found "friend" requests from both the Lady Theresa and Sir

Richard. She had also responded to his note welcoming him, pointing him to some forums she thought he might find useful, and giving him permission to claim the honor of "under consideration" to them both.

Shortly after he changed his profile status, he received a message from someone who said his name was Peter.

"Dude, you are so lucky to serve the Lady Theresa. I could never go there, I'm a total 0, but I really regret missing out on the opportunity."

Jesse wrote back, "Thanks, but what's a total 0?"

"On the Kinsey scale. When I offered myself to the Lady Theresa, she said she wasn't looking for a straight boy, so I just assumed you're serving Sir Richard as well. My apologies if that's not true."

Jesse had to look it up. "The scale ranges from 0, for those who would identify themselves as exclusively heterosexual with no experience with or desire for sexual activity with their same sex, to 6, for those who would identify themselves as exclusively homosexual with no experience with or desire for sexual activity with those of the opposite sex, and 1-5 for those who would identify themselves with varying levels of desire or sexual activity with either sex." Could he identify as heterosexual when he let a man fuck him? He certainly didn't *desire* sex with Sir Richard, but he couldn't deny the "experience with."

Sir Richard listed himself as bisexual and Jesse had now told the world, or at least everyone on the site, that he was in service to both the Lady Theresa and Sir Richard. Given that, Jesse had also pretty much told that world he wasn't straight. He changed his orientation to heteroflexible and his role to submissive, logged off, and crawled into bed.

Friday morning, Jesse slept as late as he dared and crept into the kitchen to find breakfast dishes in the sink and no other evidence of anyone else in the house. He left a vague note about spending the weekend with friends, grabbed a sausage roll, and headed for the Max.

At the end of the day, he didn't know whether to laugh or cry when the same sense of dread overwhelmed him as he boarded the westbound bus. He couldn't decide which was worse, going home to a family that didn't understand him or to a man who would use him sexually. But, when the beautiful Lady Theresa opened the door, Jesse could only fall to his knees and cover her feet with kisses. She grabbed his hair and pulled his face up to meet hers, pressing her lips to his, and he forgot about everything else. He wrapped his arms around her slender legs and clung to her until she released his hair.

"What's wrong, boy?"

Jesse bowed his head.

The Lady Theresa put two fingers under his chin and forced him to look into her beautiful brown eyes.

He pressed his lips together, unable to articulate his thoughts, his greatest fear her disapproval.

The Lady wove her fingers into his hair and dragged Jesse into the living room. She perched on the leather sofa, her knees crossed, her pretty feet tucked under her thighs. "Boy, do you know the one thing that will get you tossed from this house instantly and with no option to ever return?"

Jesse shook his head, his bottom lip trembling, his traitorous cock sticking straight up. He tried to assume the position, but the Lady still held his hair and he could only stay up on his knees.

"You can't submit to someone you don't trust implicitly, nor can any Dominant accept your submission without absolute trust. Trust is built in many ways, but communication is key. The only thing that would result in your immediate and permanent dismissal from consideration is a lie. We expect you to be honest with us and that includes sharing your concerns, your feelings, your tribulations, even if they result from things that happen outside this house."

The Lady's gaze sliced through him and Jesse couldn't lower his head because she wouldn't release his hair. As much as he wanted to, he couldn't pull even his eyes away.

"Am I gay?" he blurted out, then clapped his hands over his mouth.

The Lady laughed. "Is that what you're so worried about?"

"Yes, Ma'am."

The Lady sighed and pulled him close so he could rest his cheek against her denim-covered thigh. Jesse whimpered. He wanted this more than anything else in the world, but the price ...

She stroked his curls and he scootched closer so he could breathe in the wondrous aroma that emerged from between her legs. "At best, you might be heteroflexible. But, just because you allow Richard to bugger you doesn't make you gay. Wanting to suck his cock, yearning to take him in the ass the way you hunger for the privilege of licking me, that would make you gay, or at least bisexual."

Jesse wrapped his arms around the Lady's hips and clung to her, trying to keep his tears trapped beneath his eyelids.

"Do you know what forced bisexuality is, boy?"

"No."

"It's a fetish, one of the many Richard and I have in common. In reality, the forced part isn't entirely accurate, since consent is required at some level. But, it involves a Dominant requiring their straight submissive to have sex with someone of the same gender." She leaned down and whispered in his ear, her breath hot against his cheek. "And, you know what a fetish is, don't you boy?"

"Something that gets you all hot and bothered?" He inhaled deeply so her arousal chased away the fear of her husband's cock invading his mouth.

"Close enough." She bit his earlobe. "The fact that you don't want to have sex with Richard, but accept his cock in your ass because you know that's the only way you get to stick your tongue in me is a huge turn on for both of us." She chuckled. "In reality, the less you like it, the more aroused we get."

Jesse licked his lips. "Will I ever get a chance to be with you, without Sir?"

"As long as you accept there will be times when I'm not available that Richard will want you all to himself."

He swallowed. Allowing Sir Richard to use him sexually while he could distract himself with the Lady's soft folds and delicious ambrosia was one thing. Getting fucked in the ass without that? He shuddered.

She ran one finger down his cheek. "In time, boy. To earn our collar, you have to give yourself to both of us. We know that will take time, but you're worth waiting for."

The heady aroma emerging from between the Lady's legs made it difficult for him to absorb the meaning of her words. Not until after dinner, after the Lady beat his ass until he could only sleep on his stomach, after he licked her to three orgasms and sucked Richard's jism out of her after the man fucked them both, did he remember. Drifting off to sleep on his pallet at the foot of their bed, he heard the Lady's words in his head and their meaning embraced him. "You're worth waiting for."

"Boy, if you ever see that woman heading for the kitchen, intercept her and get her whatever she wants. Under no circumstances attempt to eat anything she prepares." Sir Richard fondled the tomatoes and placed half a dozen perfect ones on the vendor's scale. "I love Theresa dearly, but I'm not sure she could boil water if her life depended on it." He gently set the tomatoes into a cloth bag and added it to the collection Jesse already carried.

Jesse shifted the strap so that bag wouldn't bump against the one that held carrots and cucumbers. "Could we get some herbs, Sir? I saw some nice ones at the Gathering Together booth." As Sir Richard added bags to his burden, Jesse mentally calculated what he could prepare today. He hoped to create several meals the Lady Theresa and Sir Richard could eat during the week as well as tonight's dinner.

"Of course, boy. Anything else?"

"Do you like hazelnuts? And perhaps some mushrooms?"

Sir Richard smiled and turned back toward the hazelnut vendor. Staggering under the load, Jesse followed him to the last few stops and then the bus stop. Fortunately, he'd thought to wear his bus pass on a lanyard around his neck, so he didn't have to try to access his wallet. He tried to imagine what it would have been like to do the weekly shopping by himself. Of course, if he served the Lady Theresa and Sir Richard full time, he could go to the Wednesday market as well, both to reduce what he had to carry each time and to provide them with the freshest possible fruits and vegetables.

While he unpacked the bags, Jesse grouped together the items for recipes he wanted to prepare. After tossing together a quick chef's salad for lunch, he assembled three casseroles and taped heating instructions to each one. He roasted the chicken Sir Richard had purchased with garlic, rosemary, thyme, hazelnuts, and new potatoes, and sauteed mushrooms with onions and Cabernet leftover from the night before.

After dinner, the Lady Theresa allowed him to give her a massage. They kept a second table in the upstairs hall closet. Jesse set it up in the middle of their bedroom and covered it with a clean sheet. She stretched out naked on the table and for a moment he couldn't move, enchanted with her slender legs, narrow waist, and exquisite rear. He shook his head so he could focus and poured massage oil into his palm, rubbing his hands together to warm it. Starting with her shoulders, he used his finger tips and palms to knead her muscles. She was so tiny, he always worried about hurting her, but she wasn't as delicate as she looked. He massaged oil into her back, arms, and legs. Before he touched her sweet, tight ass with his oil slick hands, he covered it with kisses, gratified when that resulted in her delectable ambrosia overpowering the rose scent of the massage oil in his nostrils.

After wiping the oil off his hands, he held her hair while the Lady turned over onto her back. He drank in her slender beauty with his eyes and switched from muscle massage to sensual strokes. Starting at her neck, he licked every inch of her skin before caressing it with oiled palms, his mouth lingering on her exquisite breasts. Moments like this, he could imagine no other place he wanted to be, no other woman he wanted to serve. He yearned to spend the rest of his life doing whatever he could to make the Lady Theresa smile, to inhale her exquisite essence, to hear the enchanting exclamations that emerged when she shook with the orgasms he engendered with his tongue. He buried his face between her legs, his palms reaching up to caress her breasts, and entered an euphoria he never wanted to leave.

Until Sir Richard entered the room.

Jesse heard the man stride over and kiss his wife. She slid her arms around his neck and shook with her third orgasm. Jesse wrapped his arms around her hips to prevent her tremors from dislodging him from heaven. All too soon, Sir Richard swathed her in a blanket, propped her on the bed where she could watch, and took her place on the table. Jesse suppressed an urge to flee.

He wiped the rose scented oil from his hands with a towel and switched to eucalyptus. The Lady responded to his most delicate touch, but for Sir Richard Jesse required all the strength his hands could muster. The man worked out every day and had the brawn to show for it. Stretched out on the table, the tension in his muscles created a challenge that took all of Jesse's training to tame. He kept his lips pressed together, concentrating on his technique rather than the hard, smooth skin beneath his fingers.

Sir Richard wiggled when Jesse massaged his ass, knowing better than to skip it. By the time the man turned over, his massive cock rose up to remind Jesse of where he would finish the evening. His own cock had shrunk to post-swimming size.

Jesse tried not to grimace while he finished kneading Sir Richard's rock hard abdominal muscles and powerful thighs. He swallowed when he could no longer avoid the inevitable and slid his mouth down Sir Richard's cock. He had learned to avoid gagging by concentrating on the glans, using his tongue and sucking as hard as he could. With oil slick hands, he gripped the shaft at the base which both prevented Sir Richard from thrusting all the way down his throat and helped bring him to climax, especially when he used his thumbs to massage the man's prostate. Although he hated the hot jism that flooded his mouth when Sir Richard came, the sooner he tasted spunk, the sooner he could stop.

After Sir Richard groaned and emptied himself between Jesse's sore jaw, the Lady lifted her hands and Jesse fled to her arms. She let him rest his head between her breasts and played with his curls.

Unfortunately, Sir Richard joined them, laying down beside the Lady, drawing her into his arms and toying with Jesse's rear. Jesse cringed. Sir Richard would get it up again. The only question was whether he would fuck his wife – which meant Jesse would swallowed even more spunk tolerable this time because it would be flavored with the beautiful Lady's nectar – or ram Jesse in the ass – which allowed him the privilege of drinking her unadulterated ambrosia.

The Lady's hand drifted down Sir Richard's chest, her delicate fingers teasing him to erection. He put one hand on either side of her face, kissing her for what seemed like twenty minutes. Then he whispered something in her ear that Jesse couldn't make out. The smile she gave him made Jesse hard again, desire glistening in her eyes. She ran her tongue along her upper lip and he ached to dive between her legs again, even if that meant Sir Richard taking him in the ass.

Jesse opened the nightstand drawer and retrieved the lube and a condom, handing both to Sir Richard.

He grinned. "We'll need two of these, boy."

Jesse tilted his head to one side, unable to fathom what the man had in mind. He handed him a second condom, but Sir Richard didn't take it.

"Put it on boy."

"Sir?"

"Don't ask questions, just put it on."

"Yes, Sir." Jesse hung his head and tore open the package. Out of the corner of his eye he saw Sir Richard do the same, although it took him longer to get his own on as he'd had no reason to wear one in years.

Sir Richard pulled him up onto the bed by his hair while the Lady scooted over toward the center. "Now, you listen to me, boy. Under no circumstances are you to move unless you're told to and if you come you won't be able to sit down for a week, understand?"

"Yes, Sir." Jesse trembled. Sir Richard picked him up and set him down with his knees between the Lady's slender legs, his hands on either side of her beautiful breasts. Her nipples stared at him from puckered areola the color of light brown sugar.

"You may suck on her tits, boy."

Grateful to have something to distract him from what he knew came next, Jesse leaned over and licked the Lady's nipple, took it between his lips, and suckled while Sir Richard lubed up his ass and pushed the head of his cock inside.

Sir Richard reached around and grabbed Jesse's dick with one meaty hand. He squeezed until Jesse whimpered then pulled Jesse forward with it and pointed it straight at the Lady's soft folds. Jesse's mouth fell open and he released her nipple. Sir Richard thrust deep into Jesse's ass, shoving Jesse into the Lady's tight moistness. She gasped and Jesse moaned.

Sir Richard backed partially out of Jesse's ass and gripped his hips, pulling him back until just the tip of his penis was embraced by the Lady's heat. Over and over again, Sir Richard fucked his wife with Jesse's cock. As much as he enjoyed the Lady's embracing his rod, Jesse hated the thrust of Sir Richard's meat in his rear. His chest grazed the Lady's tits when Sir Richard pushed into him and he had to bite his lip until it bled to keep from coming inside her. She found his nipples and with a wicked glint in her dark eyes, pinched them between her thumbs and forefingers until he cried out in pain. Her eyes rolled back in her head and she trembled so long, for a moment Jesse feared that she was having a seizure. But, the warm pulsing muscles embracing his cock assured him otherwise. Sir Richard came in his ass with a shout.

They rested there, Jesse's dick still trapped inside the Lady, her muscles spasming around him. Sir Richard held himself up on his hands, his own cock softening inside Jesse's ass. "You still aren't allowed to move boy, but you may come."

The Lady clenched and unclenched her muscles around his dick and Jesse licked the blood off his lip. With a whimper, he shot his load into the rubber, weeping at the exquisite pleasure of coming inside the beautiful Lady Theresa. "Thank you, both," he managed to whisper. Sir Richard pulled him off the Lady and he lay between them on his side, Sir Richard pressed against his back, the Lady cradling his head on her shoulder.

He would never appreciate being taken in the ass or having a mouthful of cock. But if letting Sir Richard fuck him meant he could occasionally make love to the exquisite Lady Theresa, if he could serve her in all ways, he would tolerate it. This was where he wanted to spend the rest of his life.

"I love you Mistress, Master." He didn't even choke on that last word.

"We love you too, boy," they said in unison.

Acknowledgements

This book would not have reached your hands without the help of many dear friends and colleagues. I thank my readers and supporters, especially Patrick, my boy, my love, my muse, my webmaster. Thanks also to all those who have served me, well and ill, over the years. I have learned something from each one of you and I hope that you find what you seek.

Other fiction

by I.G. Frederick includes:

Complicated Couplings

Four sexy stories about tangled twosomes

"If You Love Someone" – Tara leaves her husband to move in with Nathan, but he abandons her after a few months. When he returns, begging her to take him back, life and love look very different.

"Commiserate" – The same man dumped them both. When they commiserate, they discover more in common than an ex-boyfriend.

"Passion's Price" – Richard steals Gina's heart from three thousand miles away. But, when he moves across the country, her intensity and passion for life drive him away.

"Lunchtime Lover" – Both married, they started their affair with the promise never to fall in love. Then Lisa's divorce becomes final.

www.eroticawriter.net/ComplicatedCouplings.html

Cougar Conquests

Beautiful older women on the prowl and the sweet young cubs captured by their allure

"Benjamin" — A chance meeting at a munch in a tiny town leads Benjamin to an opportunity for training. But, Lady Gina tries to end the relationship rather than emotionally torture herself.

"Festival of Eros" — The handsome young man followed her around all evening, behaving like the perfect submissive ... until she learned his identity.

"Paddles" — A biker bar with no bikers? The decor, name, and patrons of a bar in a small Eastern Oregon town puzzle William who just stopped in for a beer. Then the owner introduces him to the secrets of this very special tavern.

"Starting Over" - When her pet walked out on her, she stayed away from parties because it hurt to watch other women playing with their toys. But, a friend coerces her into attending a unique event.

"The Cougar and the College Boys" — Alone in the woods, hours from Portland, Tess discovers four college friends staying in a nearby cabin. The boys invite her to share their campfire, their dinner, and ...

WARNING:

This book changes women's attitudes about relationship dynamics, forever.

In Geneviéve's journey of discovery she dabbles in the BDSM lifestyle which forces her to recognize and acknowledge her true nature. Her memoir, woven together with that of a male slave, draws the reader into an intense odyssey of sexual expression triumphing over sexual repression while delivering fascinating insight about a different kind of love.

"The aptly titled Dommemoir *delivers on so many levels... It quickly sucks you in and envelopes you in the bondage of its spell...* Dommemoir *is a character study that breathes complex and compelling life into its hero, the devastating Lady Geneviéve and the fortunate submissives who worship at her feet... placing you in the delicious bondage of its dark and compelling landscape..."*

Larry Brooks, USA Today bestselling author of
Darkness Bound *and* Bait and Switch

www.eroticawriter.net/Dommemoir.html

Eleanor & Mick

A journey of sexual exploration and insight

In five sizzling hot stories, Eleanor seeks refuge in a small town on the Oregon Coast and befriends her younger neighbor. He captures first her heart and then her submission, taking her on a journey of sexual exploration and insight.

"Salt for His Wounds" — When Eleanor's ex-husband shows up begging for a second chance, she asks her young, gorgeous next door neighbor for a favor and Mick takes advantage of the opportunity.

"The Mercantile" — Eleanor attributes Mick's detachment to the difference in their ages, but Mick confesses a need for kink. Afraid of losing him, Eleanor reluctantly consents to bondage and pain.

"The Things We Do for Love" — When her gorgeous girlfriend visits Eleanor on the coast, Mick's obvious attraction troubles her. But, Liz only has eyes for Eleanor.

"Paid in Full" — Mick's army buddy finds Eleanor hot and makes a deal with Mick. But, if Mick really loved Eleanor would he let another man have sex with her?

"Renovations" — After Mick spends a month renovating their garage, Eleanor discovers he built in a few surprises.

www.eroticawriter.net/EleanorMick.html

Family Dynamics

Six sultry stories exploring sexuality in Dominant/submissive liaisons

"'Aunt' Grace" — Jen needed a place to stay in Portland and turned to her father's stepsister. But, she found so much more than she ever dreamed possible with her "Aunt" Grace. Second Place, NLA:I John Preston Short Story Award.

"Leather Family" — Kyle needs his own boy. Jacques would do almost anything to find a place in a Leather Family. But, Kyle serves a female Master.

"Searching"— Two dominants love each other, but need someone who submits to them both. Just how far will young Jeremy go to serve the lovely Lady Theresa?

"Taking Control" — To free the woman she loves from a horrid sadist's perverted games, Melanie must set aside her own aversion to men.

"Family Ties" — When her slave's ex faces eviction, Katherine offers refuge. But can Naomi pay the price?

"Said the Unicorn" — Tessa dedicates herself to her Master's service, so his determination to add another woman to their family devastates her.

www.eroticawriter.net/FamilyDynamics.html

Fork In The Road

Changing people's lives, and relationships in three pairs of sexy stories

"Said the Unicorn" — Tessa dedicates herself to her Master's service, so his determination to add another woman to their family devastates her.

"Proposals" — The evening appears perfectly arranged for him to pop the question. But, Christopher's proposition takes Geraldine on an unanticipated sexual adventure.

"Winners & Losers" — When he finally walks away from the blackjack table, Jeffrey finds someone worth gambling on.

www.eroticawriter.net/ForkinRoad.html

Ladies in Love

Six sizzling stories of Lesbian Lust

"Empty Seat" — Laura offers Alex a nightcap as thanks for help with a presentation to a prospective client. But they never order drinks.

"'Aunt' Grace" — Jen needed a place to stay in Portland and turned to her father's stepsister. But, she

found so much more than she ever dreamed possible with her "Aunt" Grace. Second Place, National Leather Association: International John Preston Short Story Award.

"Spa Date" — Dismayed that she introduced Sam to the woman who betrayed her, Julie tries to fix her up again.

"Taking Control" — To free the woman she loves from a horrid sadist's perverted games, Melanie must set aside her own aversion to men.

"Dental School" — How can Cindy flirt with the beautiful blonde dental instructor while her mother propositions the student examining her teeth on Cindy's behalf?

"Commiserate" — The same man dumped them both. When they commiserate, they discover more in common than an ex-boyfriend.

www.eroticawriter.net/LadiesinLove.html

Lessons Learned

Sometimes you need more than love

Four sizzling hot FemDom love stories about women who come to terms with their dominant sides and discover that makes them more attractive to the men they love.

"Tea Party" — What if the first time your best friend drags you to a FemDom "Tea Party" you see your former boyfriend serving canapes naked?

"Blind Date" — How do you respond when you find your ex-husband hanging out at the restaurant where you planned to meet your "Blind Date"?

"To Serve" — If you love a vanilla woman and you only want "To Serve," how do you introduce her to the lifestyle without scaring her away?

"Change in View" — What if a "Change in View" alters the attitude of the man you mentored so he could find his perfect Mistress?

www.eroticawriter.net/LessonsLearned.html

Love Hurts

but in a good way

five steamy stories about the dark side of love

"B&D Trainee" —Online, Xavier promised to make his B&D fantasies come true. But, had he jumped in over his head?

"Knife Play" — Seeking a knife he saw online, Jack

inadvertently found himself in a room full of pain and bondage contraptions. He almost turned around and left, but a beautiful woman taught him a different way to appreciate blades.

"Pussy Whipped" — Eric knew nothing about BDSM, but purchased a ticket to a fundraiser to help out his friends. When Miranda asks him to "play," he discovers exactly what those four letters mean.

"The Auction" —He attended the auction with only one goal — to acquire a very special whip. But an offer to try it out proved irresistible and he discovered sometimes events, and women, can exceed one's expectations.

"FemDom Fairy Tale" — A FemDom's offhand remark about a photograph at an erotic art show draws a handsome man's attention. But, when two dominants find each other attractive, which one chooses to kneel?

www.eroticawriter.net/LoveHurts.html

Second Chances

Six sexy stories about getting a second shot at the gold ring

"Back to School" — An admin error forces Jordan and Dennis to share a dorm room. Older than their class-

mates, they decide to stick together. But Jordan's past threatens to keep them apart.

"Gordon" — When the cover model of her latest book walks into the coffee shop where she writes, Lenore embarrassingly calls him by her character's name. His reaction confounds her.

"Spa Date" — Dismayed that she introduced Sam to the woman who betrayed her, Julie tries to fix her up again.

"Salt for His Wounds" — When Eleanor's ex-husband shows up begging for a second chance, she asks her young, gorgeous next door neighbor for a favor. Mick takes advantage of the opportunity.

"Proposal — Tangled Webs" — The evening appears perfectly arranged for him to pop the question. But, Christopher's proposition takes Geraldine on an unanticipated sexual adventure.

"Starting Over" — When her pet walked out on her, she stayed away from parties because it hurt to watch other women playing with their toys. But, a friend coerces her into attending a unique event. (Condensed version originally published as "FemDom Party.")

www.eroticawriter.net/SecondChances.html

When Two's Not Enough

Seven sexy ménage stories

"Tribal Fusion" — Whenever and wherever he dances, Dominic collects propositions, but the Lady Lenore's proposal takes him by surprise.

"Two Brothers" — A divorcée in a flashy sports car attracts the attention of two young virgin brothers visiting the "big" city of Boise.

"Honeymoon" — Although she expected to honeymoon aboard a cruise ship, Allison finds herself sailing on a private yacht staffed by an incredibly beautiful couple. Believing her new husband wants to hide his older, less attractive wife, makes it difficult to enjoy the hedonistic delights offered in paradise.

"Jail Bait" — Serena wants Joshua to pop her cherry, but he won't touch her because of her age. When her birthday finally makes it legal, he arranges for a very special celebration.

"Nikki's Birthday" — Even someone happy in a monogamous relationship might find the gift of a hot, new toy for an evening of decadence incredibly exciting. (Inspired by a real birthday present given to a lovely little bi-sexual, genderqueer slave.)

"Market Boy" — When a beautiful Domme offers Jack the opportunity to serve at a party for her friends, he responds too quickly and too eagerly, getting more than he bargained for.

"The Cougar and the College Boys" — Alone in the woods, hours from Portland, Tess discovers four col-

lege friends staying in a nearby cabin. The boys invite her to share their campfire, their dinner, and ...

www.eroticawriter.net/TwoNotEnough.html

Who Tops Who?

when dynamic dominants find each other irresistible

"Chocolate Cake" – Her submissive toys wait for her at home, but Louise finds an offer by an attractive Dom as tempting as Chocolate Cake. (First published in One Night Only: Explicit Erotica, edited by Violet Blue.)

"FemDom Fairy Tale" – A FemDom's offhand remark about a photograph at an erotic art show draws a handsome man's attention. But, when two dominants find each other attractive, which one chooses to kneel? (First published in Desire Presents.)

"Switch" – Liza found it difficult to maintain control around Emanuel, but she found his offer to share his slave with her irresistible.

"Theresa" — Richard admits to boorish behavior, but Theresa has no use for his apology. Then, he persuades her to accept a ride home from him and proves his integrity.

http://www.eroticawriter.net/WhoTopsWho.html

Young & Eager

Barely legal but hardly innocent

"Two Brothers" – A divorcée in a flashy sports car attracts the attention of two young virgin brothers visiting the "big" city of Boise.

"Teachers Pet" – Trapped at an all-girls' school in the middle of nowhere, Sabrina tries to get her hunky teacher to bust her cherry.

"Arresting Development" – Bethany went out with Officer Rick to avoid a speeding ticket, but discovered she enjoyed getting "arrested."

"Jail Bait" – Serena wants Joshua to pop her cherry, but he won't touch her because of her age. When her birthday finally makes it legal, he arranges for a very special celebration.

www.eroticawriter.net/YoungEager.html

Or visit

http://eroticawriter.net/

to find links to individual stories

and additional collections

and

For darker, edgier fiction
look for books by

KORIN DUSHAYL

The Darker Side
of Intimacy

transgressivewriter.com

www.ingramcontent.com/pod-product-compliance
Lightning Source LLC
Chambersburg PA
CBHW071411170626
46811CB00003B/1347

* 9 7 8 1 9 3 7 4 7 1 3 7 8 *